TO FIND A VIKING TREASURE

GINA CONKLE

To Find a Viking Treasure

The Norse Series Book 2

Gina Conkle

To Find a Viking Treasure
Copyright © 2016 by Gina Conkle
ISBN-13: 978-1542533294
ISBN-10: 1542533295

NYLA Publishing
350 7th Avenue, Suite 2003, NY 10001, New York.
http://www.nyliterary.com

Chapter One

AD 1022

Uppsala, the throne seat in the Viking kingdom of Svea

"You've been sold."

"What?" Sestra's pitcher plopped into a barrel of ale.

"To a man of Uppsala." Lady Mardred raised her voice above the din and rescued the bobbing vessel. "Or Gotland. I'm not sure."

The matron set the pitcher on a table where leeks awaited slicing. Lady Mardred cleaned her hands with quick, efficient swipes. Thralls came and went in her life. It was the Viking way.

Raw-boned men crammed into the longhouse, their coarse voices booming off smoke-hazed rafters. Warriors, farmers, fishermen. The kind of men to charge first into a fight and last to leave. All had gathered to have their say and argue who should be king. Ill-winds had come to Uppsala,

1

the throne seat of the Viking kingdom of Svea. King Olof was freshly exiled by his son Anund Jakob, but a Dane called Gorm had come, claiming he was better fit to rule.

Two men vied for the empty throne. Who would win it?

But, Sestra was a lesser mortal with a simpler question. *Who bought her?*

She stared numbly at a craggy-faced man pounding his fist on a table. One hand touched the hidden scar on her neck. The ridged skin oddly soothed her.

"You don't know his name?"

"Your mistress didn't say." The Viking matron plucked a copper-banded bucket off a high peg where eight more buckets lined the wall.

"Will I meet him soon?"

"You will," Lady Mardred said, counting earthen pitchers waiting to be filled. "Tonight, I think. But you labor for me first until all these men are fed. This is all I know."

All these men. The sea of masculine faces blurred in the cavernous longhouse. One of the men would take her. Tonight.

Lady Mardred's blunt news crushed her secret wish for freedom, so did the kingdom's troubles, but a rusted war hammer hung near the door, a heart-warming sight, and clear proof not all Vikings were blood-thirsty. Lady Mardred's husband had an aversion for war. It was his purpose in calling Uppsala's men together, a bid to peacefully choose one king.

"Sestra." Lady Mardred gentled her voice. "I need you to fill these pitchers. Can you do that?"

She forced a cheery smile. "Yes."

Hiding emotions was a skill she'd mastered long ago. Thralls, especially the women, couldn't afford the luxury of honest feelings. Those who fought didn't live long, survival had taught her as much.

"Good. The meat is almost done, and I fear if we don't feed these men soon, they won't have the patience to hear what my Halsten has to say." The tall matron walked to her cooking fire, a long gold braid swinging from the crown of her head.

Sestra dunked a new pitcher in ale, the grainy sweet aroma filling her nose. With tempers on edge, she'd have to tread with care. The turmoil could make it easier to move unnoticed, except for the red-bearded stranger from Aland. His lustful glint cut across the longhouse. The leering visitor had pawed her bottom when she'd poured his drink earlier. His breath's slimy feel still lingered on her neck when he'd whispered how he'd use her later. Thralls made easy prey for lust-addled warriors and could never refuse them.

Her grip on the pitcher's handle tightened. She was done lifting her skirts for men.

Eyes narrowed on the roomful of noisy Vikings, she hefted the vessel with too much fervor, splashing cold ale on her chest.

"Uhhh," she gasped. Gold droplets splattered her freckled cleavage. Her skin would be sticky all night.

Sturdy brown wool barely covered ample curves from an error when her mistress sized her. The poorly cut tunic brought her much unwanted attention.

"May my new lord prove generous in dressing me." She pinched the sopping bodice. If she could move the neckline a finger's breadth or two higher, she'd be decently clothed.

She crouched behind the barrel and yanked up her neckline. A stitch snapped. The strained fabric hardly budged. Chin to chest, she exhaled and tugged again with both hands, jostling her breasts for room that wasn't there. If she could tie her apron higher and shield them...

The fine hairs on her neck stood on end as a pair of familiar black leather boots cross-gartered with frayed leather stepped into view.

Brandr.

Cheeks flushing hotly, a groan caught in her throat. There was no graceful way out of this.

She released the awkward grip on her bodice and raised her head, meeting the Viking's mocking grin with a tight-lipped smile. Tarnished silver eyes pierced her from the shadows where the savage warrior stood, a thumb hooked in his belt.

"Sestra."

Her skin prickled. Brandr's deep voice marked her when he said her name, the same way a wild beast's growl did when stalking prey in a midnight forest. Strength rippled under his black tunic stretched across shoulders broad enough to block out the light. By Viking standards, he was barely tame, preferring the woods to Uppsala's people. His edge, born of a near-feral nature or simply hard man, weakened her knees. The warrior rattled her, and he knew it.

And tonight he'd sought her.

"What are you looking at?" she snapped, rocking back on her heels. It was a good effort to restore faltering confidence.

4

"You." His graveled voice rumbled with humor.

"At least we know your eyes work."

Brandr's grin split wider. "The rest of me does too, but you won't get *your* work done hiding back here."

She itched to slap the smirk off his face. Of all men, *he* had to be the one to witness her, ducking behind a barrel, ale-splashed breasts jiggling as she struggled with ill-fitting clothes.

The Viking leaned against a post, holding a drinking horn casually against his thigh. "Got a problem with your clothes?"

"I'm sure you have better things to do than worry about my tunic."

"Looked like you needed help. You usually do." He took a drink, eyeing the table full of empty pitchers and uncut vegetables.

Her knees hurt, a reminder she hunkered down on the floor. Bellows rose from the crowd and through a crack between two barrels, she witnessed two red-faced men. One banged a fist on the table, sending wooden bowls clattering against empty drinking horns in their stands. Someone needed to fill the drinking horns of angry men.

"You could be the last man standing," she said, pushing to full height. "And I'd not ask for your help."

She snatched her apron to her chest. Dabbing the excess ale bothered already sensitive skin. How was it her ears found his voice in all the noise? The Viking was never friendly.

Brandr taunted her most nights in his unhurried way, but she got him back. Spilling mead on his boots at feasts. Serving food to others first, giving his portion last. Or not at all. His self-assured gaze would follow her before the warrior got off his seat, giving her a slight nod as he ambled off to fetch his food.

Besting him thrilled her, made her blood race at their strange game of cat and mouse. Drying off her skin, she had an inkling Brandr fed on it too. Yet, he'd never groped her and never demanded she lay with him. He'd not touched her at all.

Her hands slowed on her breasts. Was that why he sought her now?

"Missed a spot," he said, eyeing her low neckline.

Her nipples pinched to hard, pebbled points as a slow trickle of wetness disappeared in her cleavage. Brandr's grin was a slash of white against black whiskers as if he knew what her body would do and wasn't disappointed. Her mouth opened with a ready retort, but she froze.

Was he the one who'd take her?

Brandr was a House Karl, a humble fighter of Uppsala. He excelled at scouting for the chieftain Lord Hakan. The role fit. Nothing escaped his keen eyes, including a wayward droplet of ale. When others bragged of their exploits, the silver-eyed Viking stayed silent. Warriors young and old nodded respectfully when he walked through Uppsala. At feasts, people always made room for Brandr on crowded benches. The rough-souled Viking kept to himself most nights, gambling with one or two others to improve his meager fortune, which gave her pause.

He couldn't be the one. He lacked adequate coin.

Brandr tapped his chin, chuckling. "Might want to close your mouth."

Her fingertips touched her lips. He didn't goad her the way he did most nights. His teasing was mild at best, but a black-eyed warrior hailed Brandr, interrupting a moment that went on too long. Dropping her apron, she exhaled slowly.

She escaped...something.

Brandr straddled the bench, a secret smile on his lips as though he read her thoughts. She leaned a hip against the barrel and smoothed her apron's pleats. *Get through this night.* She didn't have time to trade barbs with Brandr. The matter of who bought her hung over her head.

Ella, a fragile-framed thrall, balanced pitchers in both hands, wending her way around tables and men. She plunked down the empty vessels on Sestra's table. "My feet ache already and the evening's not half done."

"Then why don't we take a much deserved rest? The men aren't drinking much tonight."

"Because their tongues wag of war." Ella's blue eyes dimmed. "I've lived here all my life and never has there been fighting in Uppsala."

"I miss the old king." He at least kept the peace.

King Olof had tried to abolish the old ways of worship, but the people of Uppsala would have none of it. They wanted sacrifices of animals and men every nine years as was their pagan custom. The king's young son, Anund Jakob, swore to keep the custom the day he forced his father to leave. All of Uppsala marveled at the bloodless exile until another caused trouble. Gorm. The Dane had lurked all summer, a predator sniffing weakness, waiting for the right moment to claim to the throne.

All for the love of power and their Norse gods.

Sestra stared at the fire pit's dancing flames, remembering the day the king left Uppsala.

Water numbed her feet. Hot tears rolled down her cheeks. Throngs milled about the shore, the silence uncanny. Wood creaked from King Olof stepping aboard his ship. He gripped the vessel's dragon head, his penannular ring gleaming on broad shoulders.

Grim-faced men churned oars in water. The king faced Uppsala, watching his people with stoic eyes until morning mist swallowed him whole. One by one and two by two everyone left, their footsteps whispers on the sand until she stood alone.

King Olof, the only man to ever show her fatherly kindness, was gone.

Ella nudged her. "See how they finger their weapons."

Sestra blinked and focused on the raucous longhouse. "Because they itch to use them."

"If chaos comes, what will you do?"

"Hope my new lord takes me far from here."

Ella's smooth brow furrowed. "I heard you were sold."

Sestra gripped the barrel's edge. Laboring for Lady Henrikkson had been a gift for both thralls. The older woman was more mother hen than exacting mistress.

"You don't seem vexed by the news," Ella went on.

"There's nothing I can do about it," she said, eyeing a group of men snarling at each other.

"You could ask for your freedom."

A farmer stumbled into Red Beard, and the stranger from Aland shoved the man all the while watching Sestra the way a serpent eyes a mouse. She turned away, but his eyes burned holes in her back.

"Freedom?" Sestra's voice notched higher. "Better to serve a *wealthy* master. That means security."

One she thought she'd found serving the Lady Henrikkson and her warrior son, Sven. Lady Henrikkson was a reasonable soul, the kind of woman Sestra believed would listen when she raised the subject of her freedom.

"You don't want to be a free woman?" Ella asked.

To say no to a man? To stand as his equal and speak her mind? Viking women did, and men listened. The sight of it stunned her. No one had ever asked if she wanted freedom, not until she came to Uppsala. Nor'men and women lived with passions as sharp and bright as their long summer nights. Nothing could contain them.

Growing up a slave of Frankia formed her differently. Sex was her currency. Survival was all she knew. Yet, she loathed men handling her like common goods. Her favorite trick to evade unwanted attention, ply a man with ale until he passed out.

She winced. Sometimes the ploy didn't work.

"Freedom." The word tasted unusual on her tongue. Yes, she wanted it. Badly. But, she hoarded that truth. Life was safer if no one knew what she truly wanted. A secret hope couldn't be taken away. Scratching her thumbnail across the barrel's wood grain, she finished, "I've been a slave from birth. This life is what I know."

Ella rested both elbows on the barrel's lid, her cat-like blue eyes flaring at the sight of the man with Brandr.

"Well, if I had to be sold, I wouldn't mind belonging to him."

The raven-haired warrior diced for paltry coins. He was only a few years older than Sestra, but his handsome face bore the openness of one not scalded by life.

And like metal to lodestone, her attention shifted to Brandr.

His profile could be hewn from a distant wilderness. Harsh places had built his rugged frame. He stretched one long, muscled leg along the bench, showing trousers coarsely mended in three spots. Probably done by him. The Viking had little more than her.

"No. I need a lord dripping with gold, someone to make life easy."

"Sestra," Ella giggled. "You're a thrall."

"But a smart one." She winked and bent to fill another pitcher. "There is one thing. I tire of men grabbing me. I'd like to be free of that."

Ella looked blissfully at the roomful of warriors. "Lady Henrikkson keeps me close most nights for anything to happen."

"Be glad she does," she said softly.

Lady Henrikkson had taken Ella in as a babe. It was only natural the matron would be especially watchful of her. When male guests stayed at the Henrikkson longhouse, Lady Henrikkson beckoned Sestra to give comfort if needed.

Most thought her quick-tongued and flirtatious, but years of rutting men left her heart brittle. No man could truly touch her.

A dull ache yawned in her stomach pressed against the barrel. Memories of gentler times threaded her mind. Her mother's warm smile on a cold day. A kind touch and laughter shared. Those images frayed the way of old cloth, the cost of seasons passing.

She blinked thrice, wetness prickling her eyes. Dust must have caught on her lashes. "I say find one master who guards his house well and all others leave you alone." Her voice lightened. "Life needn't be so hard for the likes of us."

"I know what you want, less work or none at all."

Her forced grin faded. Would she ever stay in a settled home and have a place to live until her final breath?

"What about him?" Ella bumped her shoulder, her gaze sliding to Brandr. "I vow he'd guard a woman well."

"Brandr?" She wrinkled her nose. "I wouldn't want him to have control of me. He's too…too…"

"Too what? Too handsome? Too strong? Or too smart to let you lead him by the nose?"

"No. More like too big, too poor, and too…too…" She huffed, searching for the right word. "…too *hard* a man."

"For you to manage you mean," Ella said, tossing back her ebon braid. "I've heard highborn ladies whisper about him. They seem to like him very much."

A hot pang hit her. No wonder the surly Viking didn't touch her. Why would he when highborn women beckoned from lavish, fur-covered beds?

She dragged another pitcher through the ale, banging the insides of the barrel. "And those highborn ladies are welcome to him."

Brandr bent his head over the game. Light from a hanging soapstone lamp shined on black-brown locks curling at his nape. He was a rarity, a Viking with black hair cropped short. The uniqueness made him stand out among the people of Svea. Did highborn women like his hair that way?

She set the earthen vessel down with a satisfying thud. He was the wrong man for lots of reasons. It didn't matter that she couldn't put them into words.

"Ella. Come quick." Lady Mardred rose from her cooking fire, balancing a platter of meat. Lips pursed, she raised an eyebrow at the unfilled pitchers. "Sestra, serve the ale."

She balanced a full pitcher on her hip. The black-eyed warrior dicing with Brandr waved her over, waggling an empty drinking horn. A gold arm ring gleamed brightly on his wrist. A cross and sprouting plant carved the metal, the mark of the exiled King Olof.

"You're just in time," the younger warrior said when she approached. "I need to celebrate my victory."

A small pile of coins sat on the bench between his legs.

"Ah, I see you've won much tonight."

"Beware, man. A woman'll lighten your purse before they know your name." Brandr held out his cup, admiring her unbound hair. "Especially the redheads."

Her lips tightened at the slight. "At least he has something to give a woman." She softened for the younger warrior. Him she graced with her best smile. "What's your name?"

"Gunnar."

She poured his ale first.

"Gunnar." His name rolled gently off her tongue. She rubbed her hip slowly, ignoring Brandr's outstretched cup. If he painted her a heartless seductress out to fleece a man, she'd play the part.

Brandr's stare locked onto her hand stroking her hip, a dark light flaring in his eyes.

"You look new here," she said to Gunnar. "So let me give you some advice. Keep your earnings. Then you won't end up like other warriors who have nothing to show for their effort."

Brandr clutched his chest in mock pain. "Wounded by the fairest of thralls."

She took his cup, her heart fluttering a split-second. Did he think she was the fairest?

His attention dropped to her neckline. "How modest she looks tonight."

"And you look like a man running out of coin," she shot back, pouring his ale. "As usual."

"Less for a man to spend on women." His taunting grin showed white within black whiskers. It had to be several days since a blade touched his jaw.

She held out the cup, and warm calloused fingers covered hers, sending a pleasant tingle up her arm. His crooked excuse for a smile played her. Or was it the way Brandr's gruff voice stroked her skin? The Viking always sounded like he spent too much time in smoky places.

"I wouldn't know," she said, shaking off his odd effect. "Of all the warriors here, you spend only barbs on me."

"My charm's lost on you."

"*Charm?*" She huffed. "Did your mother ever teach you such a thing?"

He cradled his cup with both hands, black lashes shuttering his eyes. "That woman gave me nothing but misery."

Brandr took a long draught of ale, lost to a dark place by the distance in his eyes. She shifted the pitcher to her hip, wanting the churlish warrior back. Sparring with him was better than thorny silence. Behind her raised voices debated the merits of the old king against his usurper son.

"I'm surprised you're not giving your opinion on who should be Svea's king," she said. "Everyone else is."

"Don't have one. Don't care."

"What?" she gasped. "Have you no sense of loyalty? No sense to do what's right?"

Gunnar raised a finger. "I for one think—"

Her hand went up, halting Gunnar. "I don't believe it." She dropped onto a bench and angled herself toward Brandr.

He drained his cup and stared into the empty horn. "It's true. I'm loyal to me and me alone. Always have been."

"What about your vow of service to Lord Hakan? Isn't he loyal to the old king?"

"I don't speak for Hakan," he said, harsh lines framing his mouth. "My service to him ended at Lithasblot."

Lithasblot. The festival celebrated the beginning of harvest. Men and women considered their accomplishments and asked their gods for strength to achieve what lay ahead. Farmers culled animals deemed too weak to survive winter. Though the season of snow and ice was far off, Vikings refused to waste fodder on unworthy livestock.

It was a time of cold, hard decisions.

And while all of Uppsala had feasted, Brandr had eaten in silence that first night before disappearing into the woods until the festival passed. Now the Viking avoided eye contact, pinching his drinking horn hard enough his fingertips turned white.

"I think you to be many things," she said. "But a man without honor isn't one of them."

As soon as the words were out, she regretted them.

Brandr's jaw tensed. "Sorry to disappoint, but you won't have to think of me anymore."

She went still, her body tensing as if a blow would come. "What do you mean?"

"He leaves on the morning tides." Gunnar scooted into her side vision. "To Gotland. For good."

Brandr would be gone forever?

Her feet were planted on the floor, yet the ground could be spinning. She squeezed the clay pitcher in her lap, its coarse surface biting her palms. The weight anchored her on this night of bad tidings. To not see Brandr anymore? They didn't like each other, but there was comfort in seeing his broad shoulders in a room.

If he was nearby, she was safe.

Her lashes dipped lower at the revelation.

Brandr rested his elbows on his knees, and the iron amulet he wore swung free of his tunic. "Miss me already?"

A quiver skimmed her backside. His voice was low and there was something intimate when he leaned toward her, his hands linked together. She glimpsed skin where Brandr's tunic opened at the neck. His chest wasn't tan. Noticing the small detail struck her as seeing an inner sanctum, as personal as the scratched amulet he wore honoring Tyr. A spear had been stamped into the metal, the symbol for the Viking god of war known for courage. Yet, few spoke of Tyr. Thor, Odin, Loki, Freyja. The folk of Uppsala relished discussing those Norse gods along with tales of giants and women warriors flying across the skies.

The well-worn metal dangling from his neck captivated her, a tell-tale secret of the man who wore it. "I thought you'd stay for the fight that brews."

"You thought wrong," he said softly.

His silver stare pinned her. The moment strung tautly and for once she wished the abrasive warrior would indulge in open, friendly conversation. But, he didn't.

Gunnar scooped up his coins. "Ask him why he goes—"

"Why don't you keep your mouth shut?" Brandr sat up, scowling at the warrior.

Her gaze shifted between the two men. Did Brandr's business on Gotland have to do with King Olof?

"Even so, he who rules Uppsala rules Gotland," she said, hugging the pitcher. "Don't you care who sits on the throne?"

A tiny line cleaved the skin above Brandr's nose. "The island's far enough away."

"Not so far from here."

He rocked his cup on his thigh, the slanted indent between his brows furrowing deeper the more he held silent. The warrior cared fiercely about something. Or someone.

Why was she pushing him? She craved security but mostly the kind found by a wealthy lord who promised a safe home. Let the man she'd serve sift through the kingdom's shifting sands. Men determined war and peace, never women like her.

"Do you leave because this fight yields no gold?" she goaded. "This would be a fight for honor and the good of Svea's people."

"Careful," he growled.

"She's a woman hungry for battle." Gunnar dropped his winnings in his coin pouch. "Put her in the fight. She'd have no time to think of you."

"No." Brandr's crooked smile slid back in place. "She'll miss me."

"Like I'd miss a pebble in my boot."

But, her feeble insult had no bite. Air thrummed between them, raw and mysterious. Brandr's eyes traveled the length of her red hair to her hips. Noise faded behind her. They could be the only two in the longhouse. She sat taller under his attention, the adjustment thrusting her breasts higher.

Men's stares had latched onto her before.

Yet, none made her squirm or...*want*. Not like this.

"This isn't my fight. I've stood in the shield wall with many here." He shrugged but a bruised quality colored his voice. "It's time I leave. Make a home on Gotland."

Home.

The way Brandr spoke, Gotland could be an escape, a place he willed into existence as though any could do the same. She nodded, lost in the comforting image of an inviting longhouse on the fabled green island, but the fine image crumbled.

Brandr sought her out tonight to say good-bye.

She swallowed the lump in her throat. It shouldn't matter that he was leaving. The hard-edged warrior would sail to Gotland, and she would serve a new lord—be he cruel or kind.

Behind her, shouts rang out. Brandr sprang to his feet and reached for his sword. She twisted around. Men clamored for weapons, knocking over tables and benches. The longhouse door swung wide, a vicious war axe lodged in the wood. Blood dripped down the handle.

She jumped up, a metallic tang coating her mouth. The earthen pitcher smashed to pieces at her feet.

Was this a raid?

Brandr jabbed a finger at her. "You. Stay inside." And he ran for the bloodied door.

Chapter Two

A Norse hammer hurled end over end, splintering the lintel. The square metal head narrowly missed an eager warrior running past. Brandr rushed outside to the clash of iron on iron. Men poured around him into the yard to war cries and the crack of wooden shields.

A pair of behemoths brawled, ringed by the crowd holding pine pitch torches. He should leave, wanted to, but couldn't. He'd served both men locked in battle and like everyone around him stood mesmerized.

Two great friends warred for supremacy, but this was no friendly test of skills. Hakan the Tall and Sven Henrikkson fought wild-eyed in a struggle to kill the other.

"Ahhhh!" Hakan yelled a warrior's cry and lunged at his bear-sized friend.

Sven's shield caught Hakan's sword, the blade sticking. The bearish Viking clenched his teeth and raised his axe at Hakan.

The White Wolf, as some called Hakan for his white-blond hair, pivoted. Sword lost, his shield blocked Sven's axe and sent it spinning across the ground.

Hakan rammed his shield boss into Sven's shoulder. The giant howled in pain. Hakan's boot caught Sven's ankle from behind, and the Viking tumbled.

"Grab him!" Sven shouted, pushing himself off the ground.

Four men rushed forward. Black runes marked their yellow shields – Sig *to win* and Tyr *to sacrifice*. These were men of Aland, the island to the north. They'd come to take and kill.

Hakan knocked one fighter off his feet. His fists slammed two more warriors when Sven, breathing hard, collected his shield.

"Hakan," Sven bellowed, pointing to the outer circle where a warrior trudged from the shadows, holding a knife on a dark-haired woman. "Yield and she won't be harmed."

Hakan froze at the sight of Helena. Lady Mardred, Hakan's sister, smothered a scream. Brandr jabbed his sword tip into the earth, staunching the burning urge to slice the knife-wielding warrior. Sven could be an impulsive fool, but the bearish Viking scanned his surroundings. He had to know he was outnumbered.

Skirts brushed his legs. Sestra. *"Please.* Do something. It's Helena."

"I told you to stay inside," he said under his breath.

Of course Sestra had done as she pleased. The thrall nettled him at every turn. He wrapped a protective arm around her and spoke low in her ear. "Keep quiet. Sven won't harm Helena. It's for show. To stop Hakan."

"I'd say it's working."

The Aland warriors seized the moment, jerking the White Wolf's arms behind his back. Another man quickly bound Hakan's wrists.

"I needed your attention." Sven's breath billowed. "This was the only way."

"Holding a knife to my wife's neck? A new low for you." Hakan nearly spat the words as men shoved him to the ground. "Lower than siding with Gorm."

"*Wife?*" Sestra whispered.

Murmurs rippled around the battle circle. Brandr tried to read Sven's flinch. At the news of Helena now Hakan's wife? Or the slur at siding with the hated Dane?

"So the rumor's true." Sven bowed his head to Hakan, his arms spread wide. "May Freyja bless your home with many sons. You must agree my holding Helena gives you good reason to hear me."

Hard-eyed stares glittered from the crowd. Orange flames speared black skies from torches held high to wisely read the faces of Sven and Hakan. Men had come to decide Uppsala's fate tonight. In truth, these two lesser chieftains held more sway over who'd sit next on Uppsala's throne, and every grim-faced man gathered here knew it.

Sven shifted from one foot to the other. "The same is true for all of you," he said, his gaze roving the circle. "Tomorrow. Meet here and we'll talk of what's to come."

A few sheathed their weapons. Others cast side-long glances at dark-haired Helena, a knife gleaming at her throat. Most of the men had gone *a viking* with Hakan and Sven in times past, but Hakan's favored thrall, a woman liked by many, now held a wife's elevated status.

Nor did the White Wolf look defeated.

"Untie me and you can talk with *Solace* as much as you like."

Sven barked harsh laughter, hefting his shield with the stuck sword. "A hard thing, my friend, since I possess *Solace*."

Sestra tugged Brandr's sleeve. "Can't you do something?"

He hated getting between the two. Yet, Hakan sat hands trussed, surrounded by four men. Brandr stared at the leather ties. His own hands fisted against bindings not there. A hazy, long ago memory washed across his vision, a single thread binding him to Hakan deeper than any vow of service.

Sweat nicked his forehead. He stood on dry earth, but sensations of water creeping up his neck choked him. Mouth wide open, his chin tipped high, a reflex he couldn't stop.

The chieftain had saved him once in ways no man can count. He didn't have to do this. He'd fulfilled his oath ten-fold to Hakan, the friend who'd once cut the death bindings and rescued him years ago...the friend who now sat defenseless on the ground.

For those reasons he tipped his sword, *Jormungand* across his shoulder and stepped into the circle. "You have his attention, Sven. Hands tied behind his back, he's ready to listen. But with a knife at his wife's throat—" he nodded at Helena and all heads turned to her "—what man will hear what you have to say?"

Sven's dark eyes narrowed, likely assessing Brandr's loyalty and finding the virtue lacking. Half the crowd unsheathed their knives. Restless hands grappled axes. The whole yard teetered on becoming an all-out battle with Sven and his Aland warriors sorely outnumbered if he counted right. In these changing times, one could never be too sure.

"Why not take this inside? You and Hakan with a trusted few." Brandr glared at the warrior wrenching Helena's neck so hard she whimpered on tip toe. "And tell your man to put away his knife."

Sven scanned the yard full of twitchy men, his massive chest still heaving from the fight. "Yes. We'll take this inside." He eyed Hakan. "If you give me your word you'll listen."

Hakan's face pinched in the way of a man badly wounded, yet not a single cut was on him. His whole body strained toward Helena as if by force of will he'd save her. Brandr gritted his teeth. Was this what love did to a fierce warrior? Made him cool his anger in the dirt because he couldn't save the woman he loved? No man should be hamstrung over the fair sex.

"You have it. Let her go."

"Your bindings stay." Sven slid his axe into his belt, and he waved off the Aland warrior.

Helena slumped free, caught by Lady Mardred. Sparse words rippled through the crowd.

Much of Uppsala's turmoil could be solved by these two. None would gainsay what Sven and Hakan decided tonight. Once they were in the longhouse, Brandr would breathe easier, his obligation done. *Jormungand* stayed on his shoulder, a surety Sven would honor his word as the crowd thinned. He kept a careful eye on the Aland men hauling Hakan upright. A few more steps inside and he'd leave.

"Brandr," Hakan's voice rang out. "I need you."

A knot coiled in his chest. Beyond the crowd, three dragon ships anchored in the Fyris River, their tall masts touching the moonless sky. Come sunrise he'd be on one of those vessels and make his way to Gotland.

Two of Sven's men flanked Hakan, pushing him forward, but he broke free and took four long strides toward Brandr before the men grabbed him.

"Let him go," Sven ordered. "He gave his word."

The Aland Vikings stepped back. Torchlight glowed on the iron torque around Hakan's neck, a sign of his authority, the thing as solid as his word. Behind his proud back, leather bindings dangled to the ground.

Leather ties. A man bound without hope.

"Brandr." Hakan's ice-blue stare slid to his wife as a man dragged her into the longhouse.

Keep her safe.

Brandr rubbed the heel of his hand on his breastbone. He'd be gone come morning. Why not go inside, a last nod to their friendship?

"I'll go."

Hakan led the way, the crowd of lingering men parting for him. Warriors and fishermen alike tipped their heads in respect before disappearing. Some left on hushed feet into the dark forest. Others ranged in packs down the road, torches lighting the way. Brandr turned to follow when someone touched his arm. The freckled hand was pale against his black tunic.

Sestra.

She was another twist in these final hours. The thrall could be the sweetest tangle *if* he yielded to the urge. He nearly did. Her kneeling earlier, wrestling with her bodice messed with him made him want to steal her away and test the desires raging inside him. He liked baiting her. Sestra's quick tongue, red hair, and full curves teased his senses, always had, though he'd never let her know.

I leave come sunrise.

"Let me go with you." Her brown eyes shined softly in starlight.

His whole body went stiff. "What?" She wanted to go with him to Gotland?

"Helena's scared," she continued. "I want to help her."

Sucking in cool night air, his gaze shot skyward. "You mean go with me inside the longhouse?"

"Of course, to help my friend."

The twinge in chest tightened. The mouthy thrall cast a tender net around his cold heart. She thought only of helping Helena. He thought only of escape. Someone should warn Sestra about what was coming—about the men inside, about men like him with blood on their hands and savagery in their veins.

"And who helps you?" he asked quietly.

Sestra's lips parted. A breeze blew a fat, copper curl across her face. With her beautiful hair, she embodied *Sif*, the fertility goddess. It didn't matter that *Sif* was the shade of wheat. Sestra's red hair was made for sensual pleasure, and her body made for a man.

He yearned to bury his hands in the silken waves…to bury himself in her.

Her gentle silence was more honest than any barbs they'd ever traded. She weakened him in ways he didn't like.

He had no business asking who helped her. What waited for him on Gotland was his concern. Tonight was his farewell.

The red-bearded Aland warrior banged his hammer on the lintel. "Are you coming?"

The thick-set Viking had watched Sestra all night, lust and possession slanting his eyes. Brandr stepped in front of Sestra. The warrior smiled, a cold twist of his mouth, before slipping inside.

Brandr turned and grabbed her elbow. "Whatever happens," he ground out, "stay out of the way and keep silent."

* * *

Inside the longhouse, Helena shivered on a bench an arm's length from her furious husband. Tables were overturned. A bench snapped in two. The men of Aland kicked horns strewn across the floor. The acrid stench of charred meat mixed with spilled ale. There'd be much to clean later. For now, Sestra slid across the bench facing the center fire pit and put her arm around her friend.

Sold together at the same Frankish port in early spring, both had journeyed to Svea on Lord Hakan's ship. Helena now lived as honored wife of the man who once bought her. This was not the time to find out what happened. The sooner the men had their say, the sooner both women could find a quiet place and shut away this chaos.

The Aland warriors circled them. She huddled close to Helena, wanting to be small and unseen. Red Beard hugged his beast of a war hammer, his leer roving over her and Helena. Brandr stood near Hakan, his back against the beam.

Blood dripped down Sven's arm, likely a kiss from the axe lodged in the longhouse door. He held up a linen strip, appealing to Lady Mardred for help.

"As if I'd help the likes of you," she said, standing beside her husband, Lord Halsten.

It was bold of Sven to think the lady would render aid after he'd attacked her brother and his new wife.

Sven settled on a bench facing Lord Hakan and wrapped the cloth around his arm. "Never thought I'd see the day my friend would wed again."

"Don't count yourself a friend," Hakan said. "Gorm ruling Uppsala—"

"Gorm will not be king. He barely has control now."

"That's not what I heard."

"You heard wrong."

"And you put him on the throne," Lord Hakan went on.

"That's what I needed everyone to believe." Sven paused, using his teeth to tie off the cloth. "The Aland chieftains and I swore an oath to Anund Jakob last spring."

Lord Hakan's feet planted on stones ringing the fire pit between them. "Then why does Gorm think *you* support him?"

"We needed someone close to Gorm. It's why my men and I *falsely* serve the Dane."

"Why exile King Olof? Was Svea's peace and prosperity not enough for you?"

Lady Mardred rolled a new log onto the fire, yet a chill touched Sestra. How could she have served Lady Henrikkson all summer and not known about her son's intrigue?

Orange flames shot higher. Sven stared at the blaze, his eyes black and hollow. "We've softened. Fewer raids as in days of old. Outsiders poison our ways. And Olof declaring an end to the ninth year sacrifice?" He spat into the fire. "The sign of a frail man."

"You'd exile your king over a blood tradition? Trondheim has already outlawed the blot."

"And they grow weak," Sven jeered. "But here in Svea, blood sacrificed to Odin gave us success. *You* especially."

"No wooden statue helped me. We fought side by side, always watching each other's back. Loyalty, strength, wits. *That's* what gave us success." The sturdy bench shook at Hakan's impassioned words.

Sestra gripped Helena tighter. He didn't act like a man outnumbered with both hands tied behind his back. Sven stared into the crackling flames, his bulky frame bent under an unseen burden.

"What's your plan?" Hakan goaded. "Put a boy on the throne to keep a few worthless wooden statues in place?"

The Aland warriors grumbled, their knuckles turning white on axes and knives. One man shifted on the balls of his feet, his eyes shooting daggers. Were they going to attack because of Lord Hakan's insult?

Sven fingered the iron amulet hanging from his neck. "Anund Jakob's not a boy anymore. He's nearly your size and bearded."

"You think his size makes him fit to be king?"

"Jakob will see to it our gods stay. That makes him worthy."

Over Helena's head, Sestra looked at Brandr. The small line above his nose pressed deep. His iron-grey eyes flashed a warning. *Keep silent.*

Hadn't obedient silence always been her lot in life?

Heart racing, she flexed her trembling hand. Hemmed in on all sides, she wished for a weapon to wield at these men who took their might for granted. The vegetable knife rested beside the leeks. She'd never learned how to fight or defend herself the way some Viking women did. The want to grab the knife was foolish. Sven held the power here, yet haggard lines etched the skin under his eyes. Could it be a sign he paid a hefty price for betraying his friend?

"Jakob decreed his father can live. The old king will spend the rest of his days at your Gotland ringed fort." Sven's black stare met Lord Hakan's. "I pledge the same to you and your family *if* you help."

"The boy can't make that decree. He doesn't have control. Gorm does. And false oath or not, you dance to Gorm's tune."

"We were ready to make Jakob king." Sven slammed a fist on his thigh. "A peaceful transition. And it was for a time. That's why we waited until you journeyed to Frankia."

"Because you know King Olof is the true king."

"And you'd kill for him," Sven said, slowly. "Because of that, Olof accepted exile. He wants no more violence."

Helena inhaled soft and quick, the trifling sound enough to draw her husband's attention. His ice-blue eyes flickered when he looked at her, and she nodded, a secret passing between them. A bond tethered them implicit in what remained unsaid.

Sven cleared his throat. "As you know, the Dane returned with a few berserkers and laid claim to the throne. Men got nervous."

Helena shuddered under Sestra's arm at the mention of the fierce breed of warriors. One had attacked her late spring. Her quick thinking saved others that day, a show of courage the people of Uppsala wouldn't forget.

"Now you want Gorm gone," Lord Hakan said. "If I cooperate with you, my family and I live peacefully on Gotland. Is that it?"

A grin split Sven's bushy beard. "You always were quick to see the lay of things. Of the two problems on my hands, Gorm is one you can solve."

"If it means killing him, I'm ready."

The words slipped easily off the White Wolf's tongue. Sestra had heard whispers of a long-standing hostility between Gorm and Lord Hakan, the kind that dug in deep and wouldn't let go.

"I thought you'd be interested," Sven chuckled. "Word's already spreading that you're back."

"Where is he now?"

"Far north of Uppsala. He's moving south, farm by farm. Anyone who doesn't bow to him sees their farm burned."

"Still setting fires." Bitterness threaded Lord Hakan's voice. "What do you need me to do?"

"Keep him from burning more farms."

"And not kill him?"

Sven folded his arms comfortably over his girth. "When the time is right, you will. He has too many men. We need reinforcements from Aland first."

"You want me to lead him on a chase to buy you some time?"

"Yes. He's so blinded by his hate for you that he'll chase you through every forest and take half his men to do it."

"Leaving fewer warriors in Uppsala," Lord Hakan's voice rumbled deep and amused. "You want to divide his forces, easy targets for the kill."

"'*Never walk away from home ahead of your axe and sword.*'" Brandr. His rough voice quoted Viking wisdom.

Every male in the longhouse nodded. The words straight from Odin were bred in them with mother's milk.

"No," Helena wailed. "You can't do this."

"Shhh. It's the only way." Hakan soothed her, scooting closer to her on the bench. "We'll never live in peace until Gorm's dead."

"We must have control before the other berserkers arrive," Sven explained. "The Black Wolf of Hedeby and his men are coming. Gorm has promised them much wealth if they fight for him."

An uneasy current spread, each man looking to the other. Brutal to the bone, the cold-hearted Black Wolf was known far and wide. Born of outlaw parents, he roamed Viking realms and beyond, his lethal talents offered to the highest bidder.

"I must burn this longhouse to appease Gorm." Sven's voice boomed. "Then I'll tell him I've killed your sister, Halsten, and their daughters. It was Gorm's express wish."

Lady Mardred cried out from the shadows, but her husband stepped coolly forward. "And in gratitude we leave with our lives. Is that what you're offering?"

"You must disappear." Sven waved a hand at chests lining a far wall. "Leaving most of your wealth behind. Otherwise the Dane will question why I'm empty-handed when I see him again."

Lord Halsten's one fist curled tightly. "What better way to show your false loyalty than to give away my wealth."

Lady Mardred slumped on a bench. Sestra glared at Sven, her pulse quickening. His decree was the price paid when kingdoms crumbled, a fact she'd seen too often.

The bearish Viking looked to Brandr. "Cut Hakan free."

A home would be destroyed tonight, and the people who lived here sent away. Forever. To Sven and the Aland men, it didn't matter. Even Lord Hakan accepted this fate, his voice joining the battle plans. His zeal to destroy a long time enemy lit a fire in his ice-blue eyes.

Helena grabbed Sestra's hand, her grip shaky. Wetness splashed their fingers. Tears. The men, set on intrigue and enemies, missed the silent weeping.

Tremors shook her body as she comforted Helena, but these were not from fright. Thralls, along with the young and old, would live underfoot while warriors trampled the earth. The best of men couldn't save all the innocent from the horror.

Her lips twisted. The life of a Frankish slave woman mattered not at all.

If only she had a weapon and knew how to use it...

"You spoke of *two* problems," Brandr said, his knife sawing Lord Hakan's bindings. "If a forest chase to divide Gorm's men solves one, what's the other?"

"Find Gorm's treasure. The hoard is somewhere in Uppsala, marked by a white stone with runes painted red..."

Her head snapped up.

A white rune stone marked with red.

"...if Gorm doesn't have the treasure, the Black Wolf and his men won't fight for him," Sven finished.

"Do you know where he hides it?" Brandr asked.

"One of the islands."

Hakan rubbed his wrists. "Which one?"

She shut her eyes, fresh pain gripping her chest. The darkness couldn't stop disturbing visions from passing through her head. Farmsteads burning. Young and old put to the sword. Malevolent warriors raiding farms, snatching women and...the screams. Shaking, she couldn't block out the awful sound.

Berserkers were coming.

A white rune stone marked with red.

"The berserkers will demand to see payment before they fight," Sven explained. "If someone could find the hoard, steal it—"

"No one knows where he buried this treasure?" Hakan broke in. "Not even Astrid?"

The highborn woman known to them all shared Gorm's bed.

"Astrid told me about the stone. She fears Gorm, wants to be free of him, but she doesn't know which island."

A white rune stone marked with red.

No, the highborn woman wouldn't know where the stone rested. Sestra opened her eyes to the orange-gold blaze. Quivering chills scored her skin. This must be what happens when courage demanded action. She wanted to help, but she had no power, no weapons. She was a thrall, the lowest of the low. This was too much to ask of a woman in her position.

To speak up...to act...

Free or slave, there was no hiding. She pulled away from Helena.

"Sestra?" Helena's watery blue eyes blinked.

"Don't worry."

Lord Hakan faced her as did the Aland warriors. Sven scowled and stretched his arm to the door as if to banish her. Breathing deeply, she met his glower with one of her own.

Vikings understood one thing: boldness.

She stood tall under the weight of male stares. Brandr reached for her, but she braced a hand on his chest. Was he going to tell her to keep silent and stay out of the way?

She'd lived all her life doing that. Not anymore.

"I know the island you seek." Her voice rang clear in the longhouse. "I'll lead you there."

Brandr grabbed her, the slanted line deep between his eyebrows. "How did you gain this knowledge?"

Chapter Three

Skalds claimed Odin fashioned the earth from the remains of defeated giants. He tossed their broken bones aside, the fragments forming islands. This morning the Norse god dressed Uppsala and her islands in thick, white mist, an innocent color when blood would spill and homes would burn.

The swirling fog kissed Sestra's skin and messed with her curls, the damp air friendlier than her companion. She faced a churlish Brandr in a tiny boat cluttered with nets and baskets.

They were out to fish should anyone ask.

The Viking had showed up at sunrise with Lord Hakan at the Fyris River and swore an oath to protect her on this quest for stolen treasure for none doubted Gorm had stolen it. They were to deliver the hoard to Lord Hakan's farm further upriver where someone would wait for them. Yet, all through the stealthy journey, Brandr hardly spared a word nor did he give reason for staying.

"You missed the ship to Gotland," she said, uncoiling her braid.

"I know."

Their little vessel sliced through water, powered by muscle and sinew rippling under his tunic. The boat hugged a shoreline dense with ancient trees and mist, vigilant guards hiding sacred Viking burial mounds. Water gurgled past two weathered posts marking the Haga River, entrance to the healer's forest. Passing the mouth of the Haga, Brandr smoothly steered their boat toward open water.

She'd finger combed the wavy mass falling to her waist, the red vivid against her new black cloak. "I thought you wanted to get away from here, seek your new life on Gotland."

He shrugged, focusing beyond her. "I'll take another boat."

"If there's one to be found." Head tipped sideways, she braided her hair with practiced ease. "Don't forget you said this wasn't your fight."

The corner of his jaw ticked. "I remember what I said."

"Then why are you here?"

He squinted at her as though she'd gone soft in the head. "Because I'm looking for the treasure with you."

With you.

Her hands curled around her braid. Two words changed everything, bound them together and made them partners in this hunt. But more went on than his curt explanation gave. Brandr pulled long and hard on the oars, searching the distance, his hawkish eyes reading the mist the way others read runes. He avoided eye contact, a feat considering their knees almost touched from facing each other in the small boat.

She cast a nervous glance over the side rail. The size of their vessel on open water didn't help her confidence.

"Is that how you want this to be?" she asked, tying the bottom of her braid. "We work around each other instead of with each other?"

"I lead, you follow. That's how it'll be."

She nodded sagely at his edict, refusing to let him get under skin. "Well, you're not in this for the silver and gold. I saw your face when Lord Hakan offered the reward. You were just as surprised as I was."

"I didn't stay for the reward, but I'll take a palm of silver coins." Brandr's voice was stone rasping stone.

A palm, the Viking measurement used in trade, equaled a handful. Lord Hakan had told them upon the treasure's safe return, they could both take one palm as reward. She cupped her hand. Would she grab twenty coins? Or thirty? Under her lashes she studied Brandr's big hands wrapped around the oak oars. He'd grasp twice as much as her.

"You surprise me." Her fingers skimmed morning's vapor crowding the boat. "I'm beginning to think you are a man of honor."

Water swished from Brandr's long, determined strokes. His body flowed back and forth, a rhythm that was as calming as it was...agitating.

He glanced at her, the corner of his mouth curling up. No doubt last night's conversation crossed his mind. "Don't confuse me for a hero. Gunnar volunteered first."

"Did he? Then why are *you* here and not him?"

Brandr checked one side of the boat and levered the oar's tip on a half-submerged tree. "Never send a boy to do a man's job."

"Gunnar's hardly a boy."

"He's a whelp." He steered them around the fallen tree, his shoulder and back muscles bunching under black wool.

How was it Vikings were so big? Brandr settled the oar back in place, his gaze crossing hers with banked intensity. Warmth flushed inside her. He was muscle upon muscle, strength and bone with wet, black curls clinging to his neck.

Hard and soft.

One curl hung longer than the others. The uneven line had to be the work of the warrior cutting his own hair. Did no one take care of him?

"The whelp looked old enough to me," she said, eyeing the curl. "You expect me to believe this is about doing a good job?"

"Doesn't matter what you believe."

She leaned forward, folding her arms about her midsection. Her knees bumped the plank seat between Brandr's legs, and his warrior's thighs snapped together, a reflex she was sure, but she'd make her point. The Viking couldn't escape.

"You can try and sound as uncaring as you want, but I know better."

Brandr grunted, and she scooted back on her narrow seat. He'd waded all night through chill waters, loading the three waiting vessels in the river. During the night, many came to the river's edge pleading for a place on the ships.

News had spread quickly. Gorm was burning Uppsala with plans to set fire to all the ships.

Soon no one would be able to leave.

Come sunrise, Brandr quietly surrendered his spot to an old man. She'd surprised both men, emerging from the root cellar during their exchange. The old man raced to the ship as Brandr's silver stare challenged her to say something. Between the heavy vegetable basket in her arms and the frantic calls of Lady Mardred, she couldn't.

Now he sat with her, a riddle to unfold. And there was the reward, an unexpected boon. Like Brandr, she'd take it. Would her new lord allow her to purchase her freedom?

If they returned safely with the treasure.

She huddled on her seat. Water rippled harmlessly, darkening here, the depth too great to see the earth below. Morning would be better if the air cleared, but Brandr navigated like a man born to wind and water. She'd already described to him which island they sought when they started.

Light scraping noises brushed the boat as three gulls squawked overhead. Brandr paused to study the birds and the treetops poking through fog. A cluster of islands rose from the mist.

"Have you decided what you'll do with your gold?" she asked.

Lines framing his mouth deepened his scowl. "Do you always talk this much?"

The scraping got louder under the soles of her boots. Brandr sculled the water in long smooth strokes, checking the boat's wake.

"Yes. When I'm nervous," she said, checking the floor.

"Then you must be nervous all the time because you're always talking."

"That's different. I'm supposed to make guests comfortable at my lady's table."

The seam of his mouth tightened. "Especially the men."

She was about to give him a tongue lashing when the boat lurched violently. Heart in her throat, she gripped the side rails. "I don't know how to swim!"

"We bumped a fallen log. That's all." He dropped an oar and cosseted her shoulder. "Shhh. See there." Brandr pointed one long-boned arm at the water.

She stretched her neck for a better look, her nails digging into the boat's wood slats. The tree lay in its watery grave, a thick, green-slimed branch reaching under their vessel.

Her fast thumping heart slowed, and she let go of the rails. "Thank you for not turning that into a jest."

"You've nothing to fear. I'll take care of you."

Of course he would. He'd vowed as much to Lord Hakan. Watching over her was the Viking's final labor before he departed for better places. She couldn't let ideas about him get in her head. This surprising kindness was no different than what he did for the old man at dawn.

She hugged herself against the cold, tasting the watery air in her mouth. "I should've told you I don't like boats and deep water."

"No. You should've told me you don't swim."

Her lips wobbled with a half-smile. How like Brandr to slice the matter to its core. She'd convinced herself with fog hiding the open water, she'd be fine, but Brandr made her feel safe the moment she set foot inside the boat, his presence the lifeline she needed.

Still, her gaze skittered over the boat rail.

Brandr sliced the oars through water…back and forth, his body's motion hypnotic and smooth. "Go ahead. Talk to me."

The Viking could be a mystical warrior dressed in black against waning fog, his graveled voice working a kind of silken magic. Sun shined through clouds, the pearled orb anointing his head. Perhaps Odin did send Brandr to save the day.

Wraiths rose up from the channel as if to push them along. Did the Norse gods want them to succeed? She didn't believe in Odin and his Valkyries, but the stories Vikings spun at night entranced her.

"You could tell me what you'll do with your reward," she said.

He snorted. "I said *you* could talk to me. Not the other way around."

"That's not how it works. People take turns talking and listening to each other. It's called conversation." She angled her head coyly. "Vikings can do it. I've seen it happen."

Brandr squinted at tree tops rising above the mist. "Never been much for talk."

"Your mouth never stops when trading jibes with me."

His chuckle was raspy and low. "You have a way of loosening my tongue."

To her shame, his laugh cut a scorching path through her body and her legs fell open under her skirts. Her knees were heavy, and she left them open.

"You're a warrior long in service to Lord Hakan. Surely you'll get a bigger reward than a handful of coins?"

His tarnished silver eyes pinned her. "Maybe I get you."

She burst with skittish laughter, her nipples tightening as images of lying naked with Brandr sprang to mind. He teased her same as always, nothing more, yet she squirmed, rocking the boat, as last night's conversation with Ella came to mind.

There could be worse fates than belonging to Brandr.

"You wouldn't know what to do with the likes of me."

His smile deepened. "Give me time. I'd find a way."

Her breath hitched, and she turned her face into the cooling mist, certain her cheeks were apple red. Water beaded on her skin. She was no stranger to men, yet this rough Viking played her like a seasoned musician. Brandr lacked the smooth qualities some men naturally exuded, but a direct look, a choice word, and he strummed her senses.

And searching the water she knew. He wasn't the one who bought her. He would've said as much by now. She touched her neck, finding the ridged scar in her hairline. The unknown tortured her.

The last day she hugged her mother taught her that.

The skin she stroked thickened long ago, but memories of the Cordoba Caliphate's sapphire waters stayed tender as a new wound. She and her mother had served a Greek seller of Tyrian purple, the most sought after dye in the world. The unmarried merchant lived and breathed color, especially the gold and silver coins he counted each night by the light of his oil lamp.

"*Kokkinos*." He'd frown and wave her off. It was the name their portly master called them. Greek for red.

She'd scamper away and bury her nose in her mother's skirts. At night her mother would hold her close, whispering, "Never forget, you are Sestra."

By day their master herded hand-picked slaves to a rocky beach. There he'd stand, hands clasped over his paunch, watching over swimmers as they surfaced with a flat shell cupped in their palms. No one rested until they filled their baskets with *lapas*, the ocean creature prized for the costly purple dye.

Swimmers shouted that the waters had been stripped clean, but their master greedily sent her mother, his best swimmer, to scour the rocks once more. Waves crashed jagged cliffs dropping into azure water. Her mother's had head broke the roiling blue surface, dark red hair plastered to her skull, a pained grimace wrenching her face. From a cramp in her leg? Sestra would never know. Their master clapped his hands twice and pointed down. Her mother dove under and never came up again.

For a year she ran to the beach and stood on the shore. Cold, briny water slapped her bare feet as she stared at the same spot, hope filling her heart that her mother would pop up and swim ashore. She never did.

Loss was the open water, a still deceptive place too deep to fathom too wide to escape.

Holding out her hand, deep set lines from years of labor wrote a story in her palm. Sestra's mouth twisted on bitter truth. A Cordovan master stole her mother's life for a palm-sized creature of great value. A Viking master, she hoped, would set her free for one palm of silver and gold. But, hope was dangerous.

She folded her hands in her lap. These were secrets best kept to herself.

"You're quiet," Brandr said, breaking the silence.

"Because you prefer the sound of rowing to me."

His lazy smile spread. "Do you think me that bad a companion?"

"Worse than most," she said, smiling to soften the insult. "You taunt me for friendliness to men, but they at least talk to me."

He sculled the water, a grumbling sound rising from his chest. "Hakan and Sven agreed once Anund Jakob's on the throne, the hoard will be split among the families who've suffered. With my portion, I plan to buy sails for the ships I'll build on Gotland." His dark eyebrows rose. "Satisfied?"

"You're building ships on Gotland? I can scarce believe it."

"Believe it. I'm good at working with my hands."

Under her cloak, one hand cupped a heavy curve. Her fingers rubbed the fine wool, warmth and fullness filling her hand. *What would it feel like to have his hand on her breast?*

"And here I told you I didn't like boats," she said, her hand dropping to her lap.

"You'd like mine."

Her head snapped up. A playful light sparked his grey eyes. His deep voice, the long even strokes he took, dipping the oar in and out of water and she was mesmerized. Was the surly warrior...*flirting*?

44

"It's small boats that bother me."

The corners of his mouth twitched. "Bigger is better."

"Building boats," she said, her pulse threading a touch faster. "I didn't think your talents went beyond swinging a sword."

"Now you know I have more than one." Brandr's body flowed with easy rhythm. Masculine knees bumped hers as he rowed harder. He wasn't winded at all. Chest and shoulders swayed back and forth with each steady turn of the oars.

His pace hadn't slowed since they left the river.

Was he as unflagging in *other* exertions?

"What about you?" he asked. "What will you do with your portion?"

"Nothing. I'm a thrall, remember?"

She twirled a loose thread on her cloak. How could a woman with no control over her future make plans? She never learned who bought her. Everyone was busy saving family and goods, and Sven was too forbidding to approach. The traitorous warrior probably didn't know his mother had sold her.

Sven and the Aland warriors had circled the longhouse with torches blazing while everyone else worked fast to move people and spare belongings onto the ships. Those torches had set fire to Lady Mardred and Lord Halsten's longhouse, the flames licking home and outbuildings alike to charred ruins. Skardsbok Gard, the farm belonging to generations of Lady Mardred's family, was no more.

She eyed black smoke clouds on Uppsala's distant horizon. "Except I'm glad to stop that."

Brandr twisted around. "That'll stop soon. Hakan will make certain of it." He faced her again. "And because of you."

"Me?"

"You were the bravest person last night, standing up, telling your knowledge of the hoard like you did."

Her body stilled save her boot-covered feet rubbing at the toes. Such high praise was foreign to her ears, its source all the more baffling, yet Brandr's direct gaze was open and honest.

His boot nudged her foot. "You could purchase your freedom."

Freedom's whisper had grown stronger after Hakan offered the reward, a steady drum beat in this quest with Brandr, but she wouldn't confess the seed of hope inside her. Not to him. At least lives would be saved if they were successful.

She searched the fog. "I'm not sure. Where would I go? What would I do?"

"Those would be your choices to make."

"But a woman alone?" She shook her head. "I'd rather have a safe home where few demands are made of me."

"Freedom gives you that."

The words rolled easily off his tongue. Brandr wouldn't understand. He'd roamed the world, fighting and raiding. Two hawk owls flew overhead. The birds of prey circled and swooped, so graceful. Those two had a better chance of living in a safe home than she did, and the animals had each other. She had no one.

"There's no certainty I'll gain my freedom. A thrall doesn't get to decide how her life will go."

He scowled at her. "You believe that?"

"What else can I do?"

"Start by remembering you came into the world naked and screaming, same as everyone else. You have choices."

"You don't understand," she shot back. "I have no control over or what I do or even what I wear. And don't forget, the lord I serve decides where I make my bed."

Brandr's jaw set. "Good enough reason to fight for what you want."

"*Fight?*" she scoffed. "Just to be cut down by someone with power over me?" Her hands fisted on her lap. "I've borne enough cuts and bruises to know better."

The oars stopped. Brandr took a good, long look at her. "You're giving up."

"I'm not giving up. I'm staying smart. I learned long ago those that fight don't live long."

She sat at the edge of the bench, her heart pounding in her chest. Her rush of words said, she found herself leaning forward, glaring at the Viking.

Why did he prod her?

Brandr didn't move, holding the paddles suspended over the water. "Are you afraid to be free?"

She pushed back on her seat, his question like salt on a fresh wound. Clenched hands rubbed soft russet wool. The pretty tunic and black cloak were given to her by Lady Mardred. The tall Norsewoman loathed the idea of Gorm possessing her things, so she bestowed them on Sestra along with supple, knee-high kid boots and a small knife.

Sestra parted her cloak, and Brandr's gaze dropped to her bodice where her hand grazed the pretty neckline stitched with shiny saffron and bright blue thread. The tunic was finer than anything she'd ever worn, though she had to squeeze herself into the bodice. Her breasts caused the most comments from lust-hungry men.

One hand traced enticing cleavage, but not with seductive intent. "These are how I've made my way in the world. They're what I'm known for." She sucked in a deep breath and confessed, "I don't know what I'd do all alone in the world."

As soon as the words were out, she wished she could take them back.

Wetness pricked her eyes and she jerked her cloak tightly shut. She faced away from Brandr, not wanting the Viking to see her weakness.

"What?" she said hotly. "Aren't you going to make some jest?"

She tensed, ready for a fresh jibe to strike.

"No."

Warm tears rolled down her cheek, each salty drop pelting the unseen shield against Brandr.

"Go ahead," he said. "Let them all out. You've had a long night."

His brusque voice, oddly kind, beckoned her. She turned. Softness eased the angles of his rugged face, and Brandr rested the oars on his knees as if waiting for her.

"A good cry'll make you feel better." His crooked smile spread. "Hakan and I…we'd always have a good wallow before battle. Made us feel better."

And then he winked.

This tender humor showed a rarely seen *nice* side of Brandr. She grinned back, the abrasive warrior surprising her yet again. A few more tears fell, and her body lightened from the tiny drops rolling down her cheeks.

"It's surprising," she said, wiping away tears with the heel of her hand. "Crying does help."

A red curl came loose from the braid and fell across her cheek. She tucked the lock behind her ear.

"You have beautiful hair." His voice thickened.

She studied Brandr through wet lashes. His fingertips touched her knee bumping his, the faint contact reassuring. Often this summer past, he'd comment on her hair, but never with gentle appreciation.

"And you have much to offer—" his gaze dropped to ripe swells beneath her cloak, "—much more than your obvious charms."

Their quiet connection was fleeting and tender the way skin was sensitive from a newly healed wound, but she welcomed it, smiling brightly. Brandr sat back and dragged the oars through water, eyeing the horizon beyond her. The air was clearing.

And the rough warrior liked red hair. Her red hair.

She tugged her long, thick braid over her shoulder, the tip coiling in her lap.

"Thank you," she said quietly. "My hair is a source of pride. I'd die if it were ever shorn."

He snorted. "Like most redheads, you're a bad flirt."

"I'm not a flirt. I'm friendly."

"And for a thrall, you're pretty lazy."

Her jaw dropped. "I am not. I'm...I'm leisured. There's no need to rush through my daily tasks."

49

"Leisured." He drew the word out as if he tested a new idea. "That's what you call it?" One corner of his mouth curled up. "Tell me again how you know about the hoard."

He already knew the tale; she'd made her explanations at the fire pit last eve. Lady Henrikkson had sent her on an errand the day after the mid-summer festival. Much of Uppsala slept, and those who didn't moved on slothful feet, the cost of late-night revelry. Her task had taken her to the other side of Uppsala. Drowsy on her walk home, a shady spot along the shore beckoned her to take a nap.

Only she hadn't rested long before spying one of Gorm's ships.

He'd stopped at the island facing her. She watched a man jump out of the boat and sling two leather bags over his shoulders, one large and the other of middling size, both clinking with what had to be wealth and coin.

From the boat, two more men hauled a flat, white stone with runes painted in red.

The Dane made her neck hairs stand on end. Whatever he did on the island couldn't be for good. She'd lain in the tall grass and followed their movements through the trees. With Gorm's distinctive orange-red hair, it was easy to trace the men's movements. When they disappeared, she grabbed her basket and ran.

Brandr's low laughter pulled her back from the memory.

"I know how to keep you quiet." His smile gleamed white within black whiskers. "I'll remind you how *leisured* and *friendly* you are."

"Don't forget, my stop that day is why we're here." She leaned forward to press her point. "Many lives will be—"

Their boat lurched hard, flinging her against a basket. She grabbed the side rail. Brandr jumped into knee-high water and dragged the vessel. She spun around.

The island.

Big hands braced her ribs, and Brandr whisked her from the boat. She yelped from the shock, grappling his shoulders. Water skimmed the bottom of her boots. Then her feet were on solid ground.

Brandr waded back to the boat. He stood in water up to his knees and strapped *Jormungand* across his back. Next, he pulled an axe from beneath the baskets and tied the weapon to his thigh. The wicked iron shined against his black trousers. The curved edge had been oiled and newly sharpened.

She pointed at the axe. "Do you really need that?"

"I do. And this, too." He showed her a long bone-handled blade before he sheathed it. "And this," he said, hefting a round shield from the boat. Brandr slid his arm through straps on the back of the disc painted with wavy red and white lines, the colors of Lord Hakan.

Brandr was a walking arsenal.

He pushed baskets aside and grabbed a shovel. "But you'll need this."

"What for?"

"To dig up the hoard."

He sloshed his way onto dry land, a breeze ruffling his dark hair. Boyish mischief played on his face, and she squirmed, sand crunching underfoot. These flares of attraction needed to stop.

She eyed the shovel. "You expect *me* to do the digging?"

"You don't want to?" He tipped it across his shoulder, a smile playing with the corners of his mouth. "Not even to prove how hardworking you are?"

Lips firm, she looked heavenward. He'd baited her, jabbing at one small stain on her character, and she walked into his trap.

His smile widened. "If you and I were keeping score, I'd say I'm way ahead."

Because he was all about games.

Brandr pointed at a break in the grass near fledgling pine trees. "Would that be the way they went?"

"That is the path," she said coolly.

"Please take us as far as you remember." He bowed low at the waist. "And you can tell me all about your friendly, leisured ways."

She gathered her skirts, her footfalls digging into sand in her forward march. She taunted his gambling ways—the man had never won—before she saved her breath for the hike. Brandr stayed a pace or two behind her with the shovel slanted across his shoulder. He was alert to their surroundings, checking the area around them as she walked until they reached a split in the trail.

The island, dense with ferns and trees, was cozy. Some farmsteads with flax and barley fields were larger.

She stopped and considered the path on the right and to the left, Brandr's reassuring presence at her back. On the left, wind blew harder …the other side of the small island. A pair of squirrels raced across a tree branch. A rabbit munched on greens by a hollowed log. Nothing perilous prowled here, save the goading Viking at her back.

"This is as far as I saw," she said, the fire in her belly gone. "What do we do now?"

Brandr crouched low, his hand splayed on the soil. He studied one path and then the other, reading the earth the way old scholars studied scrolls. Men told tales of Lord Hakan sending Brandr as an outrider into remote lands in years past. They spoke with awe at his uncanny ability to read the land as if it spoke to him.

Some said he could converse in strange, foreign tongues.

How did a lowly house Karl come by such unique skills?

Brandr stood up, facing the left path. "This way."

He eyed the dirt, same as he did navigating the waterways to get them here. She fell in step behind him. The view invited shameless gawking. Black wool and leather stretched across wide shoulders. The oft mended black trousers hugged his firm, muscled bottom.

No wonder highborn ladies liked him. What woman could find fault with him? They probably ran their fingers through his black-brown hair, the only soft part on the hard man.

A pang settled in her stomach at the image of their hands exploring him. Brandr led the way aware she trailed a few paces back. The warrior didn't get impatient that her stride failed to match his. He slowed his gait on purpose.

For her.

The warrior was quick with a jibe, but he stayed quietly attentive to her needs. It was the better part of him hidden beneath his curt nature. Brandr showed startling consideration for a thrall of no importance.

Following him, she plucked a broad leaf and twirled it between her fingers. The surprising plans awaiting him on Gotland would yield great success. It was much deserved.

He was a good man.

Walking behind him in the peaceful island forest, a startling truth hit her. In the boat and on the beach, the rough Viking had teased and provoked her on purpose. Brandr challenged her to seek freedom and took her mind off encroaching fears.

She breathed easy...utterly safe and content with him.

And that was most dangerous of all.

Chapter Four

Trouble waited on this hunk of land rising from the sea. Signs of men showed everywhere. Fresh boot prints marked the soil. A charred rabbit carcass lay discarded in the grass, the faint smell mingling with damp air. Ahead, metal glinted in sand.

Brandr strode quickly to the open beach to get there before Sestra. He knelt down and wedged his shield in the earth to block the shiny piece from Sestra's view before picking it up: a fire steel, the small, flat metal used for starting fires.

Where wolf's ears are, wolf's teeth are near.

Air whispered Odin's wisdom, a reminder to keep alert.

His thumb brushed sand off the iron. The men who'd camped here made slovenly warriors. Either they didn't expect others to show or they didn't care. Were those men here now?

Or did others hunt for the hoard?

He tucked the fire steel in his belt and rose to full height, not liking unanswered questions.

His tart-tongued redhead untied her cloak, ambling past him onto the beach. If he read her right, hips sashaying, the relaxed stretch of one leg after another as she walked, Sestra was at ease. She likely missed signs of other warriors. It was better that way. He didn't want her worrying again. They needed to get the treasure and get off the island. Fast.

Sestra trudged through deep sand and turned to face the landscape. Mild waves slapped the shore behind her where seagulls squawked over a dead fish.

With her back to the open water, she planted her hands on her hips. "It's a small spit of an island, isn't it? Almost as high up as it is wide."

The distinctive crowned point made the island stand out among the few others in the waters off Uppsala. When she had described it at dawn, he and Hakan immediately knew the island.

Sestra surveyed the island's peak, red curls blowing across her face. "We should split up."

"No." He scanned dense green trees behind him and the empty beach before him. Water lapped chunks of driftwood teetering on giving up their land hold. Grainy sand stretched with natural dips. No footprints marked the beach, save Sestra's new trail.

If men used this beach, they covered their tracks well.

Sestra pointed at the path they'd trod. "That trail cuts the island almost in half. You could search one side. I take the other, and we meet in the middle."

He shook his head. "We stay together."

He pushed off the ground with his shield and made his way toward Sestra. She studied the tree line, her mouth twitching as though she judged how much time it would take to search the land.

"The island's small enough. Surely no wolves live here." She stepped to the right with an eye to a copse of pine trees. "I could go that way—"

He blocked her. "I said no."

"I'm trying to get this done quickly. Then you can be on your way to Gotland." She crossed her arms, pushing up plump breasts. "Splitting the work is pretty *un*lazy of me, don't you think?"

He stifled a smile when her brown eyes flashed hot and peevish. If they weren't careful, she'd set fire to them both. Their little sparring matches took on a life of their own. And now they were alone.

Truth trickled through his brain, bait leading him through dangerous waters.

Sunlight bounced off her coppery hair, the island's strong breeze twisting free more curls. Sestra's russet bodice strained over ripe curves. Her crossed arms was no coy move but distracting all the same. After what she'd confessed about her breasts on the boat, he taxed himself to keep his vision at eye level. Keeping his favorite redhead riled would keep her mind off the danger and away from him.

"I know why I like working alone," he said.

Her wide mouth stretched in a flat smile. "But today you're looking for the treasure *with me*."

He almost laughed at having his own words tossed back at him, except his eyes itched and his body ached. Lack of sleep weakened him. His hand gripped and re-gripped his shield's leather strap. He itched to drag Sestra off to a soft grassy place, lay her down, and free her breasts for his pleasure. He'd kiss lazy circles over plush curves and make her purr. Then, he'd wrap her cloak around them and sleep with her body flush to his.

"I gave an oath to see to your safety," he said gruffly. "I can't watch over someone I can't see. Understand? We stick together."

Sestra's arms hugged tighter all while red curls wrapped around her neck. They stood toe to toe in silence with a flock of curious seagulls watching. No warrior would question him, only a mouthy woman not used to battle. He didn't need to explain himself to her. They'd stick together because he said so.

"What about all your fine talk of choices?" Her chin tipped high. "Don't I have some say here?"

A slow smiled formed. "Sometimes a woman just needs to be biddable."

Her eyes burned a darker shade of earthy brown. "You want complete obedience."

On the windy beach, a glimmer of understanding dawned. Sestra the thrall would get feisty and grudgingly do what was expected of her, but the woman before him stepped into new waters. Sestra the would-be freewoman tried her sea legs at full-fledged independence by standing up to a man.

Warmth burst in his chest. Not just any man. She tested her independence by standing up to him.

"You want choices? Here's one for you," he said, nudging the shovel on his shoulder. "If you don't stay with me, you can do the digging when we find the hoard."

Her jaw dropped. "You wouldn't."

A deep chuckled rumbled inside him. "Try me."

Freckles twitched at the side of her mouth. Sestra measured him likely seeing how far she could push him. He didn't want to squash her will, but he stood on better ground, keeping a safe wedge between them when he was the callous brute she expected.

"I promised to bring you here and see you and the treasure back safely. Nothing about digging." He moaned dramatically, rolling his shoulder with an exaggerated stretch. "I was up all night loading ships. My back *could* use a rest."

"Fine. We stay together."

Tiredness aside, he couldn't help but grin. He shouldn't enjoy this as much as he did, but Sestra's skirts swayed something fierce when she charged across the beach to the grass.

She stopped where the sand ended and faced him, hands on her hips. "Well? Which way do we go?"

"That way." He pointed to a spot where stream and ocean met. "We follow the water to the island's peak."

Wind at his back pushed him, whispering with each long stride. *Get the Treasure. Get Sestra and the treasure safely back to Hakan's farmstead. Get on the next boat to Gotland.* His boots dug into sand and another fact hit him. He wasn't even a full day with Sestra, yet his future on Gotland drifted far from his mind.

A chill went straight to his bones. Was Odin testing him?

Green trees loomed, the heavy breeze rattling their leaves. Sun shined on his head hot enough for beads of sweat to dampen his nape. He'd do better to keep his mind on the task at hand. He scanned the path ahead, tracing a narrow break of dirt along the stream, but it wasn't well-traveled. Still, someone had disturbed the bushes. An entry or exit?

Sestra stepped sideways to let him pass, but the trail's confines pressed them close. Too close. Her breasts brushed him, the soft weight enticing. She inhaled sharply, her eyes spreading wide and pretty.

Barely tamped down sparks shocked him. His feet refused to move. Wind carried her unique fragrance, fresh warmth reminding him of farmsteads and forests. Wispy curls skimmed Sestra's cheeks, her crown of red hair beautiful against lush greenery.

Primal need surged as she tilted her face to his the way a lover awaits a kiss. Pulse pounding in his ears, his free hand stretched to touch her. Sestra's lips parted, her tender hitch of breath weakening him more than sweetly curved breasts or a brazen pout. His hand hovered between them when a warning rang in his head.

Don't ruin what waits for you on Gotland.

His hand dropped to his side. "Keep up with me."

He turned abruptly. If he gave in—and one touch was all it'd take—he'd slake his need on her. He'd make sure she got her pleasure, but afterward Sestra would look at him differently. He'd be too rough, push too hard, and she'd call him a Viking brute, same as she did other men, words he'd heard her say under her breath when *friendly* warriors reeked of ale.

The earth saved him, calming the lustful beast inside him. Forests renewed his soul the way water quenched a parched man's thirst. This was Odin's gift to him.

And his instincts about the stream were right.

The island spoke to him. Men, three at least, were here. Boot prints marked damp earth. The prints didn't point to the water as when a traveler stopped for a drink. Footfalls headed out to sea, the boot toes digging deeper than the heels—men trotting fast. Axe bites had dug into seedling trees. Someone cut bushes at the root and tossed them aside to clear part of this overgrown path.

Why here and not the other side of the island where the Dane's boat had landed?

As they walked the bank changed, becoming steeper along the water. Brambles and leaves intruded such that he pushed aside spindled branches for Sestra to pass.

"Why are we going this way?" she asked, plucking leaves off her tunic. "Don't you think the Dane would bury the hoard off the obvious path?"

"No." He was lost in reading the trail around him.

"But if he thinks no one knows about the island save the four men with him that day…" Her words drifted into silence.

He slowed down and glanced at Sestra. She grimaced at an insect on her braid, her fingers flicking the invader.

"We're here to get the treasure," he said. "Not worry about comfort."

Her lips pinched at the mild rebuke, and they forged on, discovering the narrow trail rimmed a cliff. The stream hurried over rocks below, the rush of pounding water growing louder with each step. The waterway wasn't wide but cut deep into the island. His steps stretched faster when he sighted a clearing.

Sestra hiked fast to keep up. "I can't imagine the Dane and his men working so hard to bury something they think no one knows about in the first place. This way doesn't seem safe."

He chuckled. *These men weren't bothered by safe.*

"Then don't look over the cliff."

Sestra trudged behind him, her heavy footfalls snapping twigs. "Do we avoid the island's obvious paths because you think others might come?"

Her voice wavered. Brandr stopped. He needed to concentrate and was about to say as much until he faced Sestra. Tired, insightful eyes opened to him. She was no fool. On the rare occasion other warriors spied lands with him, he never explained himself. He led, they followed. Yet, he found himself cupping her shoulder and pointing with all patience to a grassy area between trees.

"See that clearing? We stop there. It's the island's highpoint, a good place to start our search."

She inched nearer, angling for a view. Her long braid grazed his hand. The narrow trail conspired again to push them closer. Thick ferns skimmed their legs, enticing him to take a rest. Brown doe eyes framed with cinnamon lashes fixed on him, open and trusting. His hungry gaze dropped to her wide mouth and he was lost. The tiniest freckles outlined her lips save one fat mark on a corner. Temptation drew his eyes lower to a triangle of freckles on her chest.

Heat jolted his loins. The bottom tip of the triangle landed where her cleavage started.

If he laid her down, he'd suckle the freckle and smell her skin. All day.

Jewels graced the necks of highborn women, rare stones drawing the eye to high curves. No costly jewel could compete with Sestra's utterly kissable freckle.

This close, he stifled a groan. When his gaze wandered back to her face, brown lashes fluttered low. A blush stained her cheeks. Where was the thrall with the quick tongue and saucy temper? The friendly, flirtatious woman serving ale most nights at the Henrikkson longhouse was not the same woman with him now.

Sestra picked at brambles snagged on her skirt. "My new tunic…" Her words trailed off when she discovered a tear in her sleeve.

The forlorn note in her voice touched him. It wasn't simply a new tunic; it was her only tunic. Sestra was a woman who had little. Her life had never been her own. What she did here was courageous, a thrall endangering herself to save the lives of Uppsala's free men and women. No firm oath had been given, ensuring she'd gain her freedom when this was done. Hakan couldn't promise that. Sestra was giving of herself, demanding nothing in return.

And he nearly let lust get in the way.

With care, he pulled a pine needle from her hair and tossed it away. This close he saw the skin of her cleavage pebble from the gentle touch. Sestra faced him, and an ache formed in his chest. Taking a mind-clearing breath, he leaned the shovel and his shield against a tree. He surprised himself with a new want…the want to take care of her, to make her life easier.

His hands worked the tie which strapped his axe to his leg. "Tell you what," he said, striving for the careless tone he saved for her alone. "You keep quiet until I search the clearing ahead, and I'll chop all bushes and branches away to save your new tunic. When I'm done checking the area, talk all you want."

"As in ask anything I want?"

A breeze stirred leaves overhead, forest music a gentle cadence in time with birds singing their day songs. Morning sun shined on Sestra, the rays catching rare gold strands in darker reds.

"Anything," he said his voice thick.

Full breasts, red hair and you're weak as an untried warrior.

"You promise to answer me truthfully?"

"*If* you stay quiet. Including checking the clearing." Like a fool he added, "And I'll do the digging when we find the stone."

She tapped his chest, laughing. "For that, I'll stay quiet as a mouse."

The cheer in her voice warmed him better than the sun. Like a besotted fool, he smiled back and slid the shovel into the strap holding *Jormungand* to his back and hooked the shield onto the shovel's handle. He led the way, chopping branches big and small.

The trail took them to the island's highest ground where thundering water filled the quiet. A waterfall, no taller than a ship's mast, dumped into a deep, fast-moving waterway. Thick grass carpeted an inviting place overlooking the falls.

The boot prints he followed disappeared, but a few stones had been rolled away, branches unnaturally broken. He roamed the clearing's perimeter, checking the surrounding trees. Thick pines crowded together. A few Larch trees yellowed in the forest green. No well-defined path of entry existed, yet he found their exit.

Whoever had been here was gone.

His wide circle ended on Sestra spreading her cloak on the grass near a pile of rocks. She stretched out on her stomach and shut her eyes. Her head rested, cheek down, on the makeshift blanket, a picture of contentment in the sun.

He swallowed hard, blood rushing between his legs. He'd traveled far, seen places proclaimed a wonder, yet nothing could match a woman's form. *Her* form. The bow of Sestra's hips curved as lavishly as her breasts. Her full, tempting bottom arched under the wool skirt, leading his eye to the valley of her waist.

His balls ached. He willed the hardness growing between his legs gone, but resolve was a weak foe against lust. She was a thrall. He could plough between her thighs and sate his need. None would see the wrong of it.

Grabbing his water pouch, he turned away and gulped the soothing liquid. He couldn't do that to Sestra. Somewhere this summer past, through barbs and jests, he'd come to count her a friend.

A woman...a friend? He shook his head and squinted into the tangle of trees.

You're a half-wit. This is what happens when your brain falls between your legs.

A good dousing in icy water would cool his hot parts and set his mind straight. Even better, get his head on right about finding the hoard. He swiped his sleeve across his mouth and took a deep breath.

The treasure.

This hoard should be easy to find on the small island. All signs pointed to this clearing, the high ground. Grassy footprints on the first path they trod had headed in this direction.

He circled the area again, ending where Sestra rested. Ravens cawed overhead, two of them.

"Huginn and Muninn," he murmured.

Thought and Memory, the pair of birds scanned land and sea to bring back news to Odin.

Had they come to witness his choices today? He saluted the birds perched on high pine branch, smiling wryly. Of course the All-Father would be curious about his quest with a beautiful woman.

"Have some water." He dropped the pouch beside Sestra. "We may have to stay the night."

Sestra raised herself up on both elbows and drank greedily. She handed the pouch back to him, licking droplets from her lips. "You're done checking the area."

"For now. We'll rest awhile. We both need it."

Better to give in to exhaustion than his lust-strung body. He pulled the shovel from his back and dropped it on the grass under the intent eyes of his companion.

Sestra propped her chin up with both hands. "You owe me some truthful answers first."

His reach for *Jormungand* halted. The promise he'd made on the trail.

"I do." He pulled the sword free and set it beside the shovel.

Legs bent at the knee, Sestra's skirt swirled around her knees. Her boots' soft brown kid skin leather molded like cloth the length of her calves. Both feet flexed playfully, but he lingered on her leather-wrapped legs, wanting to untie the garters and kiss hidden skin.

"Hmmm…I'm not sure if I should ask how you came to speak so many foreign words or how you learned to read the ground the way you do." She plucked a long blade of grass. "But, my first question—"

"Your first of three."

"Only three?"

"I promised truthful answers. Not how many." He grinned at her and took another swig of water.

"You never said anything about a limit."

"You never asked," he said, capping the pouch and dropping it to the ground. "My offer is three. Take it or leave it."

Her cinnamon brows snapped together. Rusty laughter rumbled up inside him. Riling his favorite redhead was a sport he'd never tire of.

Sestra frowned, making the large kissable freckle by her mouth more visible. She waved a hand over the grassy spot before her. "At least sit down. Or do you plan to tower over me the whole time?"

He braced his hands on a large stone and lowered himself to the ground, his sore muscles in need of a good sauna. "A waste of a question, if you ask me. But no, I plan to rest here."

He settled his back against the rock, the early fall sun warming his face. His chest swelled with a deep, satisfied breath. Sestra's eyes narrowed on him, a perturbed cat ready to pounce, and he the mouse on which she'd feast.

"That's *not* my first question. I was showing good manners by suggesting you join me."

Face to the sun, his grin widened. "You asked a question. I answered it."

"That's not fair."

"Never said I was."

"You're using my good manners against me," she huffed.

"Everything's a weapon for the mind smart enough to see the possibility."

Sestra dipped her head and smoothed her cloak, wriggling lush curves barely contained in russet wool. Her lashes fanned freckled cheeks as though she worked a puzzle and didn't want him to see it in her eyes. Their verbal sparring matches were like a battle over the same morsel. This time he had her right where he wanted her.

He breathed easy for the first time in a long while, lulled by the waterfall's steady rush, and the companionship of a lively woman stretched out before him. If he guessed the lay of her mind, he'd say she gathered her resources, planning how to come at him with a new tactic.

"I can improve your odds." Her voice broke the silence.

His spine straightened on the hard rock. Sestra's lips curved as enticing as her words. She never disappointed him.

"And what are we wagering?" he asked carefully.

The green blade of grass tapped a smile of pure feminine satisfaction. "Ah, I see I have your full attention now."

Already strained muscles tensed. She didn't have to work hard to get his attention, but he'd be ten times a fool to admit that.

"I've gambled enough to know when to listen to a proposition."

"About that. I've noticed you gamble much, yet have little coin to your name." Sestra's eyes were half-closed, her gaze measuring him. "For all your talk about spending on women, I've never seen it. Quite a riddle you are."

"And your point is?"

"My point is you know a lot about me, and I know almost nothing about you. I don't even know where you come from."

"Is that your next question?"

She pushed higher up on her elbows, giving him a fine view of her cleavage. "I can't believe you're still counting my asking you to sit down as a question."

"Another rule of gambling: no second chances," he said, shaking his head. "Gives your opponent an opportunity."

"And second chances are a bad thing?"

"Always. Only the weak need them."

Sestra ripped the blade of grass in two and yanked up another. A pained light changed her eyes, turning the rich brown a paler shade. Their conversation struck new ground whether he wanted to or not. Sestra learned one of the hard truths he lived by, but they were here for the treasure, not friendship.

A fact his body resisted.

The richly embroidered hem of Sestra's skirt slipped higher up her thigh, revealing pretty skin above her knee. Flesh the color of cream as it turns to butter showed between russet wool and the kid skin leather boots wrapped around her calves. Would the skin behind her knee be smooth to touch?

She followed the cant of his stare. "I see you've found something to your liking."

He shrugged. "Caught me looking."

Sestra tugged down her skirt, covering that fascinating strip of flesh where no freckles daubed her thigh. "You still owe me an answer to my second question."

Her chin's stubborn angle was noteworthy. So was the inward stony shield safeguarding his secrets.

"Where are you from? And don't tell me one place," she added. "I want to know everywhere you've lived from birth to finding your way here to Uppsala."

"And here I thought you were going to improve my odds."

She swished a new green blade of grass across her lips, her eyes intent. "Answer me first."

He stared into the trees, the leaves and branches blurring. She was serious about this. Of all the questions Sestra could've asked, this one should be harmless.

It wasn't.

The rock was hard at his back, a familiar resting place for men of his ilk. He stalled, not making eye contact. The answer formed in his head, truthful words carefully plotted to satisfy the red-haired *Sif* reclining in the sun. Surely the gods tested him today.

"Born in Trondheim. Left when I was a young boy and went to Estland by the Rus. I was there a long time." He paused, crossing his arms loosely, watching her with equal interest. "Later, the Sousse seaport in the Abbasid Caliphate. From there, life on the Tigris River before I went to the Balearic Islands and then the seas...everywhere and nowhere, until I met Hakan eight winters ago."

He kept his voice level, recounting the distant lands without emotion. Sestra was all doe eyes, big and soft, when he finished. Did she read his past when he named certain places?

"Long stays in far flung lands," she said quietly. "That's how you learned foreign words."

His legs twitched, not finding his seat on the grass comfortable anymore. He hoped she wasn't showing pity. He didn't want it. Recounting simple facts, places of long ago left him exposed. Not even the sands of time could bury jagged memories. He'd told her more than he'd told the men he fought with serving Hakan.

Sestra's silence rang loud in his ears, all the more powerful for the hazy roar of the waterfall. She wanted more of him, and he couldn't give it to her.

His back drove back hard against the rock as her attention wandered over the stones around him. Her hunt for knowledge of him was at a standstill, though she pushed off the ground on her hands and knees, her braid swinging forward.

Was she going to touch him?

Arms dropping to his sides, he craved her touch. Wanted it badly. Sestra inched closer on hands and knees, hips and breasts swaying. Her hand slid along his thigh. She stretched out in the grass beside him and reached into the pile of rocks.

"Brandr, is this…" She winced, working hard, the breeze carrying her words.

Sestra wiggled against his leg. Her arm came out from the heap, the sleeve covered with dirt and broken bits of rock.

Her hand cradled a chunk of white stone marked with red.

Chapter Five

The deeper he dug, the less they found. Hours of back-breaking labor yielded coins, a necklace, two arm rings, and fragments of cut silver. A broken slab of rune stone slanted on the grass, a leather bag of middling size on top.

Sestra's eyes had lit up at the treasure, a boon for a slave to touch. Bronze coins had jingled through her fingers, and she'd held up a necklace of braided silver to sunlight. Her delight fed him, made him shovel dirt until the pit was as deep and long as he was tall.

Though neither uttered the word freedom, its spirit was in the air. Sestra's eyes sparkled differently the first moment he handed over the dirt covered bag. She'd hugged the clinking pouch and rolled in the grass, laughing with pure abandon. Her joy was the better treasure. Jaw set, he dug deeper until he stood in an empty hole higher than his head.

Sweat dripped down his temple. He jabbed the shovel into loamy soil, a faint chink of metal on metal sounding.

He dropped to one knee and his finger scratched free the last well-traveled coin. "This is the last of the loose pieces."

Sestra stretched out on the grass above him, her chin cupped in her hand. Her thick braid dangled over the pit's edge, a red ribbon against brown soil. She was richness like the earth. *Sif.*

"The larger bag's not here, is it?"

He swiped his sleeve across his face. Her spirit bolstered him, made him keep digging for the simple reward of her smile at unearthing a single coin.

"No," he said, his thumb rubbing silver stamped with a roaring lion, a coin of Thrace.

"These loose pieces have to be from the larger portion. The smaller bag was tied up well."

He balanced the Thracian coin in his palm. The rune stone was newly broken. Where the marker had been split, the rock showed clean and white.

"Could be Gorm decided it was too risky keeping the treasure in one place." Standing up, he wiped the silver clean on his tunic before lobbing it into the open pouch.

"What do we do now?"

"Take what we have back to Hakan."

Sestra pushed up on her knees. "Shouldn't we search the rest of the island?"

"It's too late." He upended his water pouch. A trickle landed on his lips.

A cool breeze blew the waterfall's mist into the clearing. The sun hung lower over tree tops, signaling the day's end. Shorter days meant fall's frost would soon come and with Gorm burning farms, the land would yield no food.

Winter would be starving time for many if the Dane had his way.

He'd hated only one man in his life. The Dane came close to making it two.

Sestra searched the dirt, hugging herself against the cold. "What happens if we return with this smaller portion?"

"Get a smaller reward? I don't know." He tossed the shovel to where his axe lay. His voice was hoarse. Weariness made his eyelids heavy.

"But we need to stop Gorm."

He laughed softly at the fierce determination in her voice. "We're not giving up. First, we take what we have to Hakan's farm."

She inspected her grimy palms. "And clean up."

Dirt smeared her skirt and sleeves. The excitement at finding the rune stone had fueled them both to tear away stones big and small. Hours of shoveling sapped his strength. Sestra had to be just as weary.

She stood up, her face sweetly streaked with dirt. "I'll get my cloak. Then we ought to go downstream and fill both water pouches."

Aching in bone and sinew, he dropped down to get the other pouch. His brain worked the riddle: the trail signs, footprints by the stream, most of the treasure missing, some left behind.

Nothing made sense.

Odin was silent. Had been all day. The All-Father preferred cunning warriors who fought all-out battles, not men who scrabbled in dirt. Salty sweat stung his eyes. He squeezed them shut and wiped, resting in the pit. Despite his hot labor, he dared not take off his tunic. Sestra could never see his back. She'd ask more questions he didn't want to answer. The redhead was growing on him; roots he'd have to sever.

He pinched the bridge of his nose. Beyond the pit, the waterfall roared, voices drifted closer, deep voices of men.

His eyes snapped open. "Sestra?"

The voices stopped.

Limbs locked, he knew. Balancing on the balls of his feet, he quietly reached over his shoulder for *Jormungand*. Grabbing air, he cursed under his breath. His sword lay beside his axe far from this hole, an error worthy of the greenest warrior. Earthen walls enclosed him. The dirt hole was the close in size to Christian burials, a fitting place for a Viking fool to die.

Smiling bitterly, he had the low ground, the worst place to be. He searched the sky above him, his ear cocked. Did they have Sestra?

"Br...Brandr..." Her voice cracked oddly.

Whoever was up there had her.

"I'm getting the water bags," he called out, stalling for sacred seconds.

His gaze ricocheted around the hole. How to save her? His knife. He pulled the blade from his boot and folded the water pouches over it. A late afternoon shadow slithered over the pit. One warrior? No. Two. Moving closer.

He inched back on the balls of his feet, out of the strangers' striking range and rose to full height. Two battle-hard men stared back. A bald, stout warrior gripped Sestra, his fat fingers digging into her arm. His other hand covered her mouth. Wide-eyed and pale, she struggled against the warrior's grip.

A taller warrior sized up Brandr, a war hammer dangling from his fist. A flat smile split his greying beard before he stepped sideways, letting sunlight blast Brandr's eyes. Brandr squinted and shaded his eyes. The taller one would die first, but he'd relish killing the stout one.

Thinking fast, he held up both hands in a friendly gesture, the pouches folded over his knife.

"When did Gorm send you to help us?" he asked, hefting himself out of the pit.

"Help you?" The tall one tapped his hammer against his leg. "Gorm didn't say anything about others being here."

"That's because you've been in the north."

The bald warrior sneered at Brandr. "Don't play us for fools. We know you serve Hakan."

"*Served* Hakan," he said carefully. "I swore allegiance to Sven Henrikkson after Lithsablot. We all know he follows the Dane."

Both men shot quick looks to each other.

"Sven sent us here on Gorm's orders," Brandr explained. "To bring back the hoard. Payment for the Black Wolf and his men."

Winds shifted with the secret said aloud. Seconds passed, marked by ravens cawing overhead and the crash of the waterfall. The bald one dropped his hand from Sestra's mouth, but he kept his manacle grip on her arm. She gulped air, her chest heaving from the effort.

The tall warrior cocked his head, his sharp scrutiny flicking from the hole in the ground to the broken rune stone. The larger piece was nowhere in sight.

76

Brandr took a casual step toward his weapons. "You can see I'm here with the Henrikkson thrall," he continued. "She guided me."

Sestra swallowed visibly, her eyes flashing split-second awareness. It was a huge gamble, hoping she sensed his plan and wouldn't crumble from fright.

She frowned at the thick fingers clamping her arm, regarding the man like an insect. "And how displeased Lord Gorm will be that you've bruised me."

The bald one sneered, "A thrall talking like a highborn lady."

"I wouldn't handle her so meanly," he cautioned. "Gorm favors her when the Lady Astrid turns cool."

"Lady Astrid is always cool," the bald one said.

She took a deep breath, her breasts testing the limits of her bodice. "Why else do you think Sven Henrikkson suggested Gorm find his comfort with me?"

The tall, bearded warrior's eyes narrowed on her. "I've never seen you with Gorm."

"Because you keep account of all the women he beds?"

His cold eyes studied her, dipping to her bodice. "I'd remember you."

Shoulders proudly back, she played to his lust. "Lord Gorm met me the day after the midsummer festival. He whispered to me of hiding his hoard here, told me he brought it that very morn with a white rune stone marked in red." Her lips pursed. "How else do you think I know of this place and the stone?"

Wind stirred the leaves and the air grew colder from the sun slipping away. The older Viking's weathered hand

77

eased its grip on the war hammer as he gave his partner a nod. The stout one let go of her arm.

"I'll keep the rest of his words to myself," she said, her chin tipping high. "Same as I'll keep quiet about your oafish hands on me, *if* you stop hindering us."

She sauntered several paces away from the two warriors, rubbing her arm, her eyes rounding on Brandr. Both men followed the sway of her backside. Sestra was panicked, but what a clever woman catching onto his ploy. He gave her the subtlest nod, acknowledging her quick thinking. She managed to remove herself a safe distance with nary a drop of blood spilled.

He still had his vow to fulfill. The treasure.

"What about the larger bag?" he asked.

The tall one's hoary brows slammed together. "What about it?"

"It's not here."

The tall one froze in place, a cool breeze twirling the pointed end of his beard. "Because it's somewhere else," he said slowly. Too slowly.

Cold sweat pricked Brandr's scalp. The giant war hammer twitched against the tall one's leg as if the weapon itched to crush bone. Brandr's thumb pressed the knife's elk bone handle hidden by the pouches. Loud cawing pierced the air. Two ravens perched high, late-day sun blasting the birds with orange light. Shadows waxed longer in the cool the clearing. Night was coming.

"Look." Brandr nudged his chin high, his blood pumping fast. "Huginn and Muninn come to call."

Gorm's men looked up at beady black-gold eyes peering down from high above. A man's life could change in the space of one look, one breath. Nostrils flaring, Brandr took his fill of island air and seized the chance Odin gave him.

Now! The word bellowed in his head.

Savage force thrummed his body. In a split second, he ducked low. Grabbing Sestra's cloak, he sprang up and threw it at the tall one's head.

"Wha—" the warrior sputtered.

Brandr drove his knife into the man's belly and turned the blade inside unwilling flesh. The drinking pouches bunched around the elk bone handle as wetness bloomed like spilled ink on wool.

Grey Beard knocked the cloak away, a snarl twisting his lips. Eyes bulging, his face was a hands breath from Brandr's. The warrior's fast, coppery breaths blasted Brandr. The man's head shook as he gaped at the knife pinning the cloak to his body.

Brandr yanked the knife free, the familiar metallic taste of battle his tongue.

Grey Beard snapped out of his shock and roared a battle cry, *"Ahhhh!"* He swung his hammer.

The iron arced wide at Brandr. He dropped low, and air whooshed over his head. Coming up fast, he jammed the blade into the man's belly again. And again. And again.

Kill or be killed. The words blasted in his head.

Blood and spittle bubbled from Grey Beard's lips. Life blurred in thin slices of act, react.

Air shot in and out of Brandr's lungs, each breath sharp and hard. *Jormungand* lay on the ground, a silver streak in green grass. The stout warrior dove and grabbed the treasure, his other hand clamped around Sestra's wrist. She fought hard, her nails scratching his face.

Sestra. Her screams rang in the clearing as the stout one dragged her away, but the tall Viking was still standing.

"You!" Teeth bared, the older warrior wobbled. Arm shaking, he swung the hammer sideways.

Brandr leaped back. Too late. A metal corner knocked his mid-section.

"*Ooomph.*" He buckled at the waist, his hand hovering over white-hot agony bursting inside him, the cost of his hesitation on Sestra.

Momentum swept the war hammer wide. The warrior's gut was unprotected. The man's poor aim would cost him. Chest heaving, unnatural calm filled Brandr. Time slowed, a gift to get his bearings and kill these men one at a time. Saltiness dripped into the corner of his mouth, his body reminding him he was alive.

The older Viking stared at spots of blood on his belly. He staggered, as sweat streamed into his beard. The hammer wavered in his grip. Brandr picked up *Jormungand* and finished the grizzled warrior with a final death thrust to his gut.

Sestra?

Battle-born frenzy thrummed inside him, but his limbs froze at the sight of the stout one holding Sestra.

The man held a knife to her throat across the clearing, three red claw lines on his jowl. Calm, ugly plans formed, plans for the man's slow, agonizing death.

The stout one jammed the heavy bag at Sestra. "Put your hand through the strap."

With one jittery hand, she tried to obey. Wet locks hung over her eyes from vapor clouding Sestra and her captor. Her skirts shook, she trembled so badly. The warrior clutched her forearm, and the leather bag banged her legs, the treasure jangling as the man forced her hand through the loops.

Brandr stalked his prey on careful feet, his sword swiveling in his grip. "What kind of warrior hides behind a woman?"

"A smart one." Fat lips peeled back into a cruel smile. "Lay down your sword."

"What's your plan? Run?"

"With the woman and the hoard." His beefy arm shackled Sestra's waist. "Once I'm in my boat, you might get her back." He chuckled coldly. "Or not."

Sestra cried out, which fed the stout one's glee.

Brandr grit his teeth. "Better to stand and fight. Run from me and you'll die a tired man."

"Not if I have your weapons." The warrior shuffled backward. He wrenched Sestra, his knife pointing above her collarbone. The tip nicked skin near her life vein.

"Brandr!"

"Quiet." The man jerked her at the waist before jutting his chin at Brandr. "The sword. Drop it."

A bright red drop beaded on the knife at Sestra's neck. The sanguine drop slid the iron and dripped over the Viking's knuckles.

"*Don't* hurt her," he ground out.

Mist touched Brandr's face. The waterfall pounded. *Jormungand*'s leather-wrapped grip, the iron guard touching his thumb and forefinger warmed him.

Wetness trickled off the man's bald pate. "If you don't want her cut, drop the sword."

A strange push-pull nagged him. He'd never yielded for a woman. Never. Sestra's whimpers wrenched him. Animal need demanded her safety. To protect her at all costs. None would lament this man's death, but Sestra…

He tensed from head to toe. Yielding *Jormungand* was a hefty price. One he was more than willing to pay. Nodding, he lowered the sword to his waist and set the flat of the blade on one palm, resting the hilt on the other. Arms outstretched, his steps careful, he could be a holy man presenting a worthy offering.

"Here. It's yours."

The warrior's eyes lit brightly on the iron. *Jormungand* did shine beautifully in twilight. Brandr stepped closer, knowledge dawning as he watched the bald one's greedy gaze.

"You're not here to get the hoard for Gorm. You're here to steal it."

The stout one snickered. "You made it easy by doing the digging."

"*The cattle are like their master,*" he quoted Odin's wisdom. "You're stealing from Gorm, the master thief. And the larger hoard? Where is it?"

"Don't know." The warrior licked his lips, his attention on *Jormungand*. "There's a rumor Gorm buried the larger portion somewhere in the healer's forest."

By the ancient burial mounds, a place of mystical power.

"He thinks the gods will protect it," Brandr scoffed, taking another cautious step forward.

He checked Sestra. She gaped at him, the whites of her eyes huge. The hoard swung from her wrist, and her body quivered as if she'd just walked out of icy waters.

He took another half-step. "It's been said Ulfberht himself crafted *Jormungand*. I was told the famed smithy labored for days on the engraving alone."

"I've heard of your sword."

"Then you've heard of the Frankish blacksmith."

The man snorted. "What warrior hasn't? He made the best weapons when he lived."

"His name is here. By the hilt." He raised the blade higher on outstretched hands and took a half step closer on muddy ground. "You need to know the serpent tale. It's etched in bronze. In the fuller."

Brandr angled *Jormungand* higher. The last trace of daylight flashed on a serpent threading through runes in the fuller, the sword's center trench, the artistry a sight to behold. The warrior's mouth gaped before he tore his gaze away.

"Play the skald for another." Colorless eyes squinted at him. "Don't come any closer, or I'll cut her."

The warrior's feet shifted closer to the cliff, thick mud sucking the soles of his boots.

"It's said in battle, the serpent uncoils from the iron." Brandr raised his voice over the pounding waterfall. "The ancient words might save you. Release the Henrikkson thrall, and I'll tell them to you."

The warrior howled brash laughter. "You must think me twice the fool. I've said it enough times. Drop the weapon."

Vapor dripping down his skin, Brandr began a slow crouch to surrender *Jormungand.*

"That's it...put the blade on the ground," the man cooed.

Huginn and Muninn squawked overhead. Did they disapprove of his fine offering? No warrior of any stature would yield his weapon to a lesser man. Better to see the sword destroyed than have its magic fall in the wrong hands. His mouth firm, he accepted the gods would judge him accordingly.

The stout Viking fairly drooled at Jormungand, relaxing his grip on the knife at Sestra's throat. "So beautiful," he crowed. "The serpent—"

"Bites!" Brandr yelled, springing up and smashing the hilt against the man's temple.

Blood and spittle sprayed into the mist. The waterfall roared as if the island demanded it's due. There was no chance to think, each movement, each expression a sliver in time.

Sestra shrieked. The knife skittered down her tunic to the ground. Brandr hurled *Jormungand* aside. The stout warrior stumbled, his feet slipping on the cliff's slick edge. Eyes rolling back into his head, his grip on Sestra wilted.

The bald man dropped into the watery chasm.

Sestra's body lurched in the thief's wake, the clanking treasure bag swinging wide, dragging her to the muddy rim. Eyes round with horror, she reached for Brandr. He lunged for her, but his foot slipped.

"Sestra!" His knees and chin slammed on mud.

Mouth open in a silent scream, she fell off the cliff.

Chapter Six

Ice cold and wet, all ten fingers hung onto a long, slick root growing out of the cliff's wall. Her body swayed from the tumble, jagged rocks and a dead man waiting below. The bald Viking's body listed in the stream, his head turned with an ill twist. The fall wasn't so deep, but jumbled rocks jutted from water as sharp-edged as a giant beast's teeth.

The island wanted to devour her flesh and bone.

She shivered, yet her heart burst with the will to live. Soaked from head to toe, her dry mouth opened. "Br…Brandr?"

Rocks and mud sprinkled her face.

"Grab my hand!" Brandr flattened his body along the cliff's rim, his arm extended to her.

Air heaved in and out of her lungs. A shot of hope surged her veins at the sound of his voice. Neck craning and blinking fast, she squinted through specks of dirt at the face above her.

The rugged Viking never looked so good.

Water thundered around her, the fall's droplets slapping her cheeks. She licked life giving dampness across dry lips, and one shaky hand uncurled from the root. She stretched for him.

Brandr inched over the cliff, grasping, straining.

"Goh!" The foreign word ripped out of him.

A narrow gap separated his hand from hers.

Her fingertips shook from straining to touch him. Her other hand slid down the slimy root as it wilted under her weight. "I'm slipping!"

Yelping, her stretched arm dropped. She seized the tuber with both hands at its thickest part, her breath coming in snatches.

"Hold on." Brandr leaned his body further out.

Mud clods rained down on her. Ducking chin chest, she shut her eyes and waited for the dirt to stop pelting her head. This couldn't be the end. She wanted to live, wanted more than a slave's mere existence. Yet, when she opened her eyes, the dead Viking stared back, water bubbling over his gaping mouth, the fast flowing stream tucking the fur cloak under his chin like a blanket for a long night's sleep.

The unnatural sight strangely beckoned her to gawk.

"Sestra. Look at me." Brandr. His voice was strong. Commanding.

Her head lifted sluggishly. She blinked slowly, her body heavy and drained. Up all night and helping Brandr today, her body had little left to give. Above her, fierce eyes promised she'd escape as if he were a host of warriors come to her rescue and not one man.

"I'm, I'm so cold." Her voice wobbled.

"Don't give up. Reach for me." Fingers splayed, his hand came closer, raining bits of dirt on her face.

She tasted earth and the tang of copper on her tongue. To save herself, she'd have to try again. One trembling hand let go of the root. She reached higher, bracing the soles of her feet on the cliff. Brander's fingertips brushed hers.

Snap.

She screamed, her body teetering wildly battered by water and the earth wall. Both hands grappled the ivory-colored stem, its flesh splitting in the thickest part.

"The root...it's breaking!"

A wave of dizziness hit her. Swallowing down bile, sharp pain lanced her shoulders. A hard lump jangled against her ribs. The hoard. The bag swung, its weight shackling her wrist.

"Sestra, try again," Brandr called out above the roaring water. "Reach for me."

"I, I can't...the treasure." Breath huffing, she glanced at the bag. "It's too heavy."

"Drop it."

Her head snapped up. "We'll lose it."

"It doesn't matter," he said, sharply.

She blinked at him. Twilight outlined the Viking, shadowing hard features as her mind raced through the facts. The hoard veered below, a bulky weather vane buffeted by wind and water. Its jingling noises taunted her not to let go. Lower still, fast flowing water jostled the dead man. His body would soon journey to deeper waters beyond the island, but she was alive

And she possessed the treasure.

"I can hold. You…you find a safe place to jump in then wade upstream to me." Her gaze shot wildly around her. "I'll drop it down to you."

"What? And wait for me to race back with a rope I don't have?" He bit out the words. "Don't be a fool."

"But…our reward."

Brandr's mouth twisted harshly as if he swallowed another of his foreign curse words. "Sestra, do you understand? The fall. You won't survive."

How much longer could she hold?

Feet numb, needle-sharp coldness crept up her legs. Frigid droplets rained down on her body, turning her wool tunic into a heavy weight. Sharp pain burned her arms and shoulders already exhausted from hauling stone. One hurt stung deepest, her vanishing freedom.

And she was supposed to drop the treasure? Simply let it go?

More dirt rained down on her. She hung in a half world, the choice, her future, balanced in her hands. Freedom on one hand or the life she'd known in the other. A thrall from birth, few decisions had ever been hers to make, yet this single moment belonged to her.

Above her head, Brandr's hoarse voice rasped, "I want you more than the silver."

Such potent, ache-filled words. No man had said anything like that to her.

Ever.

Brandr reached for her again, more of his body hanging over the cliff. He'd plunge into the ravine if he wasn't careful. A lump thickened in her throat. He risked his life to save her. In the water below, the center of the pool was calm. She glimpsed Brandr's reflection, his reaching for her.

Courage was a gift given to the man or woman brave enough to grab it.

Giving a jerky nod, she chose to be one such woman. "You're right." Her lips trembled. "I know you're right. I need to let go of the treasure."

"Keep your eyes on me. I'll guide you."

Numbly she obeyed. The whites of his eyes were bright in the darkness, but his voice was the rope she needed. Strong, a fighter to the end, Brandr would not give up on her.

He pointed at a fist-sized tip of a rock sticking out of the cliff. "Brace your foot there."

She lifted her leg, sopping wet skirts clinging to her skin, and one foot found purchase on the bumpy earthen wall. The waterfall thundered behind her, spraying her head, her back.

"Let the bag fall from your hand," he said.

Arms shaking, she pressed her cheek against the cold cliff. "My one hand…I'll have to let go."

"You can do it."

She gulped air. Her hand dropped to her side, slamming the bag against her leg. The root shook and blood rushed her ears. Wriggling her wrist, the leather strap slid over her hand, pinching the skin to shades of purple-red.

"That's it. Keep going," the Viking crooned encouragement.

Her face crumpled at the bag's slow descent. The treasure jangled innocently, inching its way down her leg as a haze of loss engulfed her. Her mouth opened wide for a deep wail building inside her. The roiling ball of loss welled up from the pit of her stomach, its hard lump rolling on through her chest to her throat.

"Go on," he pleaded. "Don't give up."

Fresh sweat beaded her forehead. A piece of silver glinted through a rip in the leather, the metal winking at her, a conniver persuading her not to let go. Eyes stinging, her lids fluttered low, surrendering her to blessed blackness. She didn't have to watch her future fall away.

Grainy straps slipped to her fingers, fingers curved in a hook not ready to let go. The old bag wouldn't withstand the sharp rocks. The silver would scatter in deep, watery places, gone forever.

"Let it go, Sestra. Let it go."

Her forehead bumped the cliff wall. Muscles cramped her shoulders. She swallowed hard, her mouth sticky and dry. Words echoed in her head.

A lifetime of enslavement...

Opening her eyes, she let go.

The hoard dropped, taking with it her muted sob. A metallic clink sounded, the treasure hitting a rock. Below her dangling feet, the bag split open and silver coins sparkled everywhere, beautiful as stars clustered in darkness. The half-full leather bag tipped over onto a piece of drift wood battering the rock.

Without the burden, she was lighter, and oddly, freer.

No pieces of silver could compete with life.

She sucked air the way swimmers did after coming up from a long time under water. Their open mouths devoured life-giving air, a thing she'd seen often sitting safely on the Cordovan shore. Now hanging from this cliff, she lived it, finding a hunger for what could be hers.

Was this what happened when courage demanded action?

Her heart drummed inside her chest, and she wanted to laugh. It took standing up to a roomful of battle hard Vikings and falling off a cliff to learn this truth. Taking a calming breath, she angled her face to Brandr where he waited, his arm outstretched. The warrior was ready to rescue her body, but no man could save her life.

Free or slave, she'd have to save herself.

"Sestra," he called out. "What are you waiting for?"

"I'm coming." Hand over hand she inched back up the thick, half-broken root. The toe of her other boot chipped away at the cliff, making a crumbly foothold. Today wasn't the day to yield her body to the earth.

"That's it. You're almost there." Brandr's voice was a prayer above her head.

Life surged through her veins. She gripped the root's unbroken part jutting from the dirt and pushed herself up with one hand while reaching for Brandr with the other. His calloused skin felt good touching hers. His big palm skimmed lower, clamping her arm as though he'd never let go.

Her breath came in fits. She clawed the earthen wall with her free hand, sending chunks of mud flying past her. Both feet toed the wall. She fought for every inch, arms and shoulders screaming in pain. Brandr lifted her little by little, the sinews of his neck standing out in full relief. His metal amulet swung free of his tunic. The spear of Tyr. Courage.

She fed on Brandr's will, locking onto the spear etched in iron. When she was close enough, he grabbed her other hand. The grip crushed her bones. Her body smashed against the cliff.

The firm line of his mouth, the hard set of his eyes, nothing was stopping him from getting her back on solid ground. Grass and level ground came into view. With a final heave, Brandr hauled her into the clearing and jerked her upright.

Face to face they stood, panting hard, a vaporous cloud billowing around them. Mist dripped down the Viking's cheeks. Twilight blurred the clearing darkly around Brandr, creating a colorless dream world save his intense silver eyes. Light-headed, she needed her bearings, she needed...

Brandr yanked her against the wall of his chest. "You're alive," he whispered into her hair.

She melted into him. Dirty, cold, drenched to the bone, there was no better place to be than in his strong arms. His warrior's heart banged hard against her ear. For her.

They clung to each other.

Wet. Shaking. Needy.

The Viking brushed mud and hair off her cheeks, searching her face, drinking in every detail, treasuring her. Long fingers warmed her jaw, discovering each slope, smoothing away damp hair. Carefully, slowly, his mouth covered hers.

The first touch stole her breath.

Brandr's lips were soft. Tender yet hot.

His long, reverent kiss melded into another kiss. Deep. Seeking. So gentle was he, the over-sized warrior could be in awe to have his lips on hers.

Sparks tingled across her skin, each hot ember sharp and bright as flares from a smithy hammering molten metal. Her nipples pinched against wet wool. Brandr anchored her in a half-world of swirling need and emotions. The seam of her mouth opened, and he moaned when their tongues touched. For all her experience, the carnal nature of their kiss shocked her to her toes. She craved Brandr, his taste, his strength. She wanted to cosset him to soothe the dark, unknown places lurking inside him.

She wanted him inside her.

Icy water drenched her, the cold droplets prickling tender skin, yet her blood flowed like hot honey through sluggish limbs. She slipped one hand under Brandr's muddy tunic, and hard male flesh pebbled against her fingertips.

Brandr broke the kiss, his breath hitching sharply. His mouth hovered over hers as if the enthralling inch between their lips fed a deep need.

His firm flesh twitched under her palm. "Your hand..." he groaned.

"Is on you," she finished, brushing her lips on his.

Was the hard-souled warrior starved for touch?

Foreheads and noses brushed as she pushed his muddied tunic up determined to have her way with him. They stood in soggy ground, not caring that they were mere steps from the cliff. Dirt smeared Brandr's furrowed midline. Taking her time, she wiped the grime off smooth skin and a weave of muscles knotted under her hand. Enveloped in darkness, her senses came alive, touching a ridged scar on his chest, smelling pine on his skin, the uneven cadence of his voice as he whispered her name against her lips.

She sought the curve of his ribs, sliding her hands to his back—

"Sestra. No." Brandr jerked away, his voice ragged.

"Why…why'd you stop?"

It was all she could do to form the question. She still tasted him on her tongue when he let her go. They stood, both breathing hard. Brandr tugged down his tunic, a bulge tenting his trousers. The waterfall crashed behind her its blast matching the uproar inside her.

Brandr picked up his sword from the mud. "We aren't safe here."

"Dead men don't care that we're kissing." Arousal flooded her body the effect better than the finest mead.

He chuckled dryly and wiped the weapon clean across his thigh. "No, they don't," he said, sheathing *Jormungand* across his back. "But, we need to get off the island and your clothes are soaked. They need to come off."

"Most men say that come nightfall," she teased. "The clothes coming off part."

He went still. "I'm not most men."

Though it was night, she saw Brandr clearly. Wet black hair fell around his face, the jaggedly cut ends grazing his jaw. The rough-hewn Viking stood like a wild beast in a rare tame moment. His tarnished silver eyes pierced her, left her tongue-tied because she put him with other men who used thralls for their pleasure.

What stopped him from taking her?

"Come," he said gruffly, grabbing her wrist to lead her away from the cliff.

Following his broad shoulders, a sweet pang filled her. Men didn't concern themselves with a thrall's comfort and certainly not a slave woman's tender feelings. Yet, this abrasive warrior did, and it touched her. Brandr led her around the open pit, his boots leaving large footprints in the loamy soil he'd dug up earlier. She planted her footsteps alongside his for the pleasure of seeing their boot prints together. Frankish maids wove love garlands made from spring wildflowers. Couldn't she be fanciful once?

Brandr let go of her when he came to his weapons in the grass. He knelt down, his profile severely set. "We need to get you to Hakan's farmstead quickly. One of the women can tend you there."

She rubbed her arms briskly. "Your warming me sounds like a better idea," she said in her sauciest voice, eyeing the bulge between his legs. "Your body agrees with me too."

The Viking turned to strap on his axe, but not before she caught his quick smile and a dimple on his black-whiskered cheek. The kiss marked him as much as it did her. Despite the day's troubles, she didn't want this time with Brandr to end. Sweet night sounds filled the clearing, of Brandr rustling in the grass, collecting his weapons, of insects and night birds and the waterfall's steady rush.

Taking a deep breath, her face tipped to the star-washed heavens. Air felt good in her lungs. Inside her chest, her heart beat steady, everything open, flowing fast. "Why do I feel so alive right now?"

"Because you cheated death."

"I feel unstoppable."

Brandr stood up, his shield strapped to his left arm. "All warriors get these high spirits when they're victorious."

"What do they do about it?" She smiled and tucked loose curls behind her ears. Of course she knew. Freewomen and slaves alike gossiped about fighting men and their particular needs after a victory.

Brandr's mouth firmed. He waited, his tolerant stare the same as what she'd seen him give to young, untried warriors. "We are getting off the island. Someone else will help you find warm, dry clothes."

"So concerned with my clothes." But her teeth started chattering.

He grasped her by the shoulders and walking behind her, steered her to the trail. "Because your lips are turning blue."

"You could warm them again," she said, over her shoulder.

They stopped by a fledgling pine tree by the trail where she turned to face him. Brandr folded his shield arm before him, setting a wood and iron barrier between them. If she didn't know any better, she'd think he couldn't wait to be rid of her. Yet, his gaze devoured sodden skirts clinging to her thighs, wandering up the length of her to land squarely on a tear in her bodice.

Bold fingers touched the shield boss, tracing the iron's curved head. "Like you I'll be glad to get away from here, but what about the hoard? Don't you think we could try to get it? It landed on driftwood."

"Which carried the pouch to deeper waters, scattering coins on its way." Brandr's eyes narrowed on her wayward hand, and his shield arm dropped to his side. "We're not chasing a few, meager coins."

Teeth chattering, she hugged herself for warmth since a dead man lay atop her cloak. "We're already wet. If we went downstream—"

"I said *no*. The treasure's gone."

Her shoulders drooped as Brandr strode back to the clearing. Standing at the trailhead, the stream bubbled gently below. The height was great but fewer rocks menaced the waters here. Bravery surged in her veins. The elation made her feet fidget and she didn't care that she was freezing.

"We came to stop the Dane, remember?" Brandr yanked her cloak out from under the dead Viking's body. "Part of the wealth is lost to him. He can't pay men with coin he doesn't have."

Gorm. The Berserkers.

She faced the waterfall. Brandr's words weren't meant to chasten, but a taste for freedom had grown strong fed by the exhilaration of climbing up the cliff…and his kiss. Being here wasn't about her. They were on the island for no other reason than stopping the coming berserkers. The reward, like their unexpected kiss, was a tantalizing side promise, and now they'd leave empty-handed.

Grass crunched softly. When she looked up Brandr blocked out the stars, his lashes black crescents on his cheeks. Silently, he reached around her, covering her with the ruined, bloodied cloak. A groan rose in her throat, and she pushed away the heavy wool about to tell him she didn't want it.

"This will help," he said, tucking the ends into her icy hands. "For the ride back."

Mud and water plastered his black hair to his skull; he had to be miserable, though he didn't complain nor was he shaking.

"What about you? You're as bad off as I am."

"I'm used to it." His graveled voice was tired. The quest finally sapped the inexhaustible warrior, or he was simply done, ready to be relieved of his vow to protect her and leave Uppsala for good.

Without a word, they turned and headed down the trail, her shoulders drooping. The trek was easier since Brandr had already cleared it. Though fatigue seeped into her bones, her mind spun with lively thoughts. On the heels of Brandr's leaving would be the coming of her new master. She wasn't the same woman anymore in part because of the rough Viking before her. She followed him, her heart fracturing with each step. He journeyed on, the shovel and *Jormungand* slanted his broad back, having no idea the turmoil inside her.

Once on the beach, Brandr guided her along the island's inner path. Night creatures stirred in the dense forest, and the sure-footed Viking dressed in black ranged the furrowed trail as if he were one of them. She retraced her morning steps led by the glinting iron shield boss swinging at Brandr's side. Finally, her legs about to give, welcome sounds of water lapping the beach came. They pushed past trees to the first beach where their boat waited.

With a gaping hole in the side.

She pulled the ruined cloak tighter, unable to ward off an icy chill. Brandr charged across the beach and crouched beside the small vessel, swearing under his breath.

She dropped to the ground, her soaked bottom landing on a patch of grass bordering the sand. "We're not leaving the island tonight, are we?"

Chapter Seven

"The hole isn't the worst problem." His hand grazed wide indents on the beach. "The other vessel is."

A six or eight man boat by the keel width imprinted in the sand.

"What vessel?"

Wiping his hand on his knee, he studied Sestra huddled on the grass. "The one that brought the two dead men. It's gone."

She blinked glassy-eyed, the haze of cold and shock depleting her. Limb-weakening exhaustion eventually followed the thrill of victory. The best of warriors fell prey to this state, and Sestra was untested in such matters.

Tomorrow she'd wake up ravenous, but tonight brought new trials.

"There was at least a third man. He left," he explained, eyeing the placid water. "But he'll return." *Looking for his friends and a treasure hoard.*

Across the channel dark trees kept vigil of who came and went. Kneeling on the beach, an unseen burden weighed on him. The island, Sestra, the hoard all made some kind of ordeal from the gods, and he the hapless learner was unsure what he should know.

He dragged both hands through his hair, ending with a hard tug at his nape. The crows at the clearing, Odin's silence, and now this damaged boat...the gods tested him with one question.

How badly did he want what waited for him on Gotland?

Wind rippled across water stretching between the island and Uppsala's mainland, a distance less than a pilskudd, an arrow shot from where he crouched. He could swim the channel and make the long midnight run to Hakan's farm up the Fyris River, but Sestra would be alone all night. With the hoard lost, he had one oath to fulfill— bring the Henrikkson thrall back safely. His heart beat fiercely with the need to protect Sestra. He couldn't leave her.

Gingerly, he tested the jagged hole. Across the beach, freckled knees showed pale above kidskin boots. From her seat on the grass, Sestra hiked her skirts up and wrung excess water on the ground beside her. He shamelessly ogled the shadowed space between her thighs when needle sharp pain pricked his finger. His hand jerked off the boat.

Holding out his hand, a drop of blood welled where a splinter gouged. He chuckled without humor. The gods demanded their due. He pinched off the sliver and flicked it to the ground. The day had its strife, but trouble of a different nature got under his skin, sweet flame-haired temptation delivered by the goddess Freyja.

Sestra meandered onto the beach. "What do we do now?"

He reached into the boat and grabbed a small leather bag. "Same as before," he said, tossing it onto the sand. "Get you warm and dry."

Tautness spread in his abdomen. He'd be the one to take care of her, and there was one best way to warm her body. He unrolled his hudfat and draped it over her shoulders. Big brown feminine eyes sought him, large and appealing.

"Your sleeping fur," she murmured, one hand stroking the heavy patchwork of pelts. "Of course you'd have it with you since you're leaving."

Gotland. The green isle had slipped far from his thoughts. Being with Sestra filled him, took up every corner of his mind. He strode to the water's edge, shaking off the revelation. Toes digging into the sand, he pushed their boat across the beach, surprised to see another pair of hands grab the rail beside him.

"Why are we moving this?" Her face contorted as she strove to match his strength.

The unwieldy hudfat hung off her frame, the bottom skimming the ground. Pale-faced, Sestra's trembling stopped, but blue tinged her lips.

"We're hiding it." With a final heave, he heaved the vessel into the reeds.

"You're afraid someone will steal our little fishing boat?"

He dusted off his hands, his ribs expanding from labored breaths. The fire steel he'd found when they arrived flashed across his mind. This morning he'd stuffed the piece away to shelter Sestra, but the brave woman he saw in the clearing deserved the truth.

"If someone passes by tonight, sees the damaged boat, they *will* come ashore." He slung his leather bag over his shoulder. "You should rest."

"I'm not a highborn woman to sit aside and do nothing," she said, planting a hand on her hip. "I can help. You know I can."

Sestra tried for her usual brazenness, but sleepy-eyed and draped in his bulky fur she was no more ferocious than a kitten. She stood her ground, red curls falling free around her mud-smeared face. He stood squarely before her, breathing scents of fresh water and clean earth from her skin, good smells to a man who preferred forests to longhouses and women doused with scented oils.

In a moment of weakness, he tucked the fur's open ends over her breasts. "It pleases me to take care of you."

Sestra's lips parted and starlight showed an entrancing indent on her bottom lip. How easily his mouth had fit there. It could again. If he kissed her, he'd test the tiny dip with his thumb, gently stroking her lip and the tantalizing freckle at the corner of her mouth. He'd not rush; he'd savor every part.

"All this time I thought you couldn't wait to be free of me," she said, her honest brown eyes searching him.

His pulse quickened, spreading molten heat through his chest, landing hot and hard between his legs. Sestra embodied Odin's test, the one woman he had no business touching, yet his hands rubbed the fur over her nipples as if he had every right to her. And by the cadence of her breath, a tender flame kindled Sestra's flesh hidden under layers of fur and wool.

If he didn't take control of his impulses, he'd steal more than a kiss.

With a slow growl, he let go and slid the bag off his shoulder. "If you want to help me, take this and wait by the pine tree."

She took the humble leather pouch. "What is it?"

"All my worldly possessions." His voice was raw and mocking in the dark.

Sestra tested the weight easily with one hand, her cinnamon brows furrowing. "How is it a warrior of your stature and experience has so little?" Her gaze touched *Jormungand's* hilt over his shoulder. "Yet you possess the finest of swords."

"Maybe I stole it?"

"Maybe you did," she said softly. "By strength alone you can take what you want."

Challenge lit her eyes. The flame-haired thrall dared him to spill another truth about himself. Why did she want to pry open his deepest places?

"I'm good at taking what doesn't belong to me."

Sestra's mouth curled in a tolerant smile when he glowered at her breasts swelling under his sleeping pelt. Fur lay flat where his hands had pressed the pelt.

She touched his arm and he nearly jumped out of his skin, the pressure of her hand palpable against his leather arm brace. "You're good at a great many things, raiding, scouting, rescuing a woman dangling from a cliff."

"But never enough to keep a woman."

A thick red curl blew across her mouth. "I've never known you to want one."

Behind him, water tapped the narrow shoreline, the rhythm of time and tides, a gentle going in and pulling out. Were the gods taking turns testing him? He was sure the wind carried Freyja's seductive laughter. The goddess could laugh all she wanted. His will would be stronger.

He gave Sestra a tight smile. "Could be my lack of wealth."

"Because you gamble away what you have. Of course, you're short on coin." She stepped closer and the hudfat brushed his thighs. "But you're rich in a good many things far better than silver."

His chest swelled under the unexpected praise. Her eyelids drooped as if the day drained her last ounce of fortitude, and she turned, carrying his things at her side, silently picking her way across the sand. This had to be a sign of trust, this change from their usual jabs. Or she was too exhausted to insult him when she had every opportunity to cut at his weakness? Sestra had to be coming off the elation that coursed her veins in the clearing.

He snapped off a branch from a bush, his body tense with unwelcome urges. Losing himself in labor, he swept away their footsteps from the beach until he reached the grass where Sestra waited. With light scarce, he squatted at the pine tree's roots.

This was for one night only. Any reasonable man could resist a woman's charms for one night.

Scanning the heavens, he scooted around the tree on the balls of his feet until he found the perfect spot where sunlight would burn brightest tomorrow. Hands flat on the trunk, he felt his way up until his palms found stickiness.

At last the island offered him a gift.

With his axe, he skimmed off a section of rough bark, exposing pale pine flesh. The blade bit bare wood with sharp slanted jabs. Nine slashes, a worthy number. Odin would be pleased. The tree's life blood shined on the light. He'd had enough for tomorrow.

Behind him dried pine needles crackled under footsteps. Sestra. Head bent, she inched into his side vision. "What are you doing?"

He took her hand and dabbed stickiness on the back. "Harvesting resin to fix the boat."

She stifled a yawn. "You'll repair the hole tonight?"

Grim-faced, he stood up and took his bag from her. There'd be no avoiding what was to come. "No. Tomorrow. Now we need shelter."

The bag slung over his shoulder, and he led her into the forest not far from the boat's hiding place. Wet clothes stuck to his skin, but he'd not build a fire. He couldn't risk someone seeing the smoke, but fire was the least of his concerns.

With one hudfat, there was one best way for two cold bodies to get warm.

Ferns brushed their legs, the tendrils thinning in a ring of trees, their refuge for the night. Covered in his sleeping fur, Sestra perched on a fallen log while he collected large branches under her watchful eye.

"Do you need help?" she asked around a wide yawn.

"No," he said, dropping his third armload of wood. "This will go faster if I work alone."

He rammed one makeshift pole after another into soft, willing soil. Sweat pricked his hairline, the labor taxing him in the best way. Grinding wood into the earth diverted his lust, and set his mind on the right course. They'd sleep here. Nothing more. He slanted one row of branches into the other row, nestling the top leafy ends in a point. Their rough abode would protect them for the night and was wide enough for two if they slept close.

"I've never seen the like before," she said, her voice floating behind him. "Yet another talent."

He faced her, motioning to the inside. "This captures our heat."

Sestra could be an elfin forest creature watching him from the log. Tales abounded of fair forest maids stealing a man's life force. Other stories told of men falling prey to their forbidden love.

Teeth grinding, he knew where he'd failed Odin's test. The kiss. He hungered for another taste. If he was an honorable man, he'd promise to protect her forever, but he wasn't a good man, never had been. He'd stolen and killed for himself and in service to others. Blood ran thick on his hands. Facing Sestra in the pitch dark forest, he felt her trust in his bones.

She was ripe for the taking.

Folding his arms across his chest, there was only one way to resist her charms. In his rudest voice he said, "Everything wet. Off. Now."

Silence.

Sestra's head cocked at an angle. Scant starlight filtered through the trees, the faint glow crowning her red hair. He opened his mouth to repeat the order, but she stood up, shrouded by branches and ferns, more mythical forest woman than thrall. A small animal stirred in the underbrush beside her, its eyes glowing between fern fronds. The little beast's courage didn't surprise him as few people ventured here: fright wouldn't be natural. Sestra lived in a different world filled with dread, yet her feet stayed in place as if she debated the merits of obeying his command. Or she debated the merits of him.

The worse she thought of him the better.

"I don't like repeating myself, but since you're a mere woman and weak at that, I'll make an exception." He paused before finishing tersely, "Take your clothes off."

Sestra put one leg in front of the other, twigs snapping with each measured footfall. When she got an arm's length from him, the hudfat dropped with a quiet *thump*.

Tension coiled low in his trousers. Eyes burning holes in him, she gathered her russet skirts at her hips. He locked onto her hem's rise, hungrily following it inch by inch. With a murmur of cloth on cloth, Sestra pulled the tunic over her head. The garment coming off was a necessary thing, not meant to be seductive, but it was.

An unseen manacle squeezed his chest when she stood before him clad in wet white linen clinging to her curves, her long braid a rope between her breasts. Round nipples jutted against the cloth, the nubs of flesh plump and red as rose hips needing to be sucked. His wolfish gaze devoured her, straining to see in the dark what he'd imagined all summer.

"Here." A ball of damp cloth slapped his chest and chin.

He deserved that. Stifling a smile, he clamped the tunic under his arm. "Now your undergarment."

"You want me completely naked?"

Heat singed his loins. Those words and the pretty O her mouth made pushed him to a sharp edge. He fought the push-pull of wanting to touch her, knowing he shouldn't, and lost. His free hand grazed her shoulder and her breath caught. The sound made his balls tighten.

He pinched the thin sleeve. "You heard me. All wet clothes. Off."

She glanced at the shelter's narrow opening. "I understand the wet tunic, but my undergarment?"

"At the clearing, you were all too willing to take my clothes off," he jibed, a fine throb growing between his legs.

"I *liked* the man at the clearing."

His chuckle rasped harshly. "You've got this one now."

An owl sang his night song overhead. Fern fronds wavered from animals scattering. Sestra's head shook as if she tried to read him and found herself befuddled. He was sure her eyes shot daggers.

"Don't talk to me like every other lout," she snapped.

An angry Sestra was good. She'd revile him.

"Keep testing me and I'll tear it off," he said with quiet menace. "Remember, I could make you go naked."

Her chin dropped bit by bit. Cruel slave traders stripped women bare, stealing their dignity, yet somewhere in this quest, he and Sestra became partners. Equal. His rough-shod words set her squarely back to where they began—thrall and freeman.

"You don't respect me at all."

He winced. Pain slanted the shape of her eyes and her voice, the smallness of it, nearly stole his resolve. No words could undo this course. He was a lout for staying in Uppsala when he should've gone, for thinking he could set aside this want for Sestra while watching over her, and then sail off to Gotland. Jumbled, uncertain words filled his mouth like loose wool skeins tying up his tongue. Her sadness crushed him, yet he stood limbs locked.

The man Sestra needed the most protection from was him.

She tossed back her braid and yanked the fragile white linen over her head. "You want my undergarment? You can have it." She jammed the limp cloth into his hand and folded her arms over her breasts. "I should never have let you kiss me."

"Thralls don't have a choice."

Her mouth flattened in an unforgiving line. "Such wisdom from the man who spent all morning telling me I have choices."

He put a death sentence on what was started in the clearing. Or tried to. Sestra bare-skinned in a dark forest stirred him better then ermine and silk. The craving for sex, for her, was winning over the need for sleep. Women were creatures he appreciated, tarried with for a time, and left. Some highborn, some not. She was a slave, and he'd admit they formed a friendship. Tonight he stood captivated by a lowly thrall, wanting to bury himself deep in the cradle of her hips.

What he wanted, he could never have.

Sestra gripped his forearm and crouched to the ground in front of him, her head brushing his knees.

Air hissed between his clenched teeth. "What are you doing?"

"Untying my boots." She let go of his arm, sharp humor edging her voice. It was the tone she used when serving ale to other men. "You did say everything wet comes off."

Tortured by her rustling against his leg, he forced himself to stare into the distance.

"What about you?" she asked. "Your clothes are almost as wet as mine."

"Not so wet," he groused.

She made a humming sound, the kind of noise a woman makes when she tolerates a man's foolishness. If his clothes came off, there'd be no barriers. He grimaced, unable to stop tension pooling between his legs. Even Sestra's little crooning did things to him.

His trousers bulged uncomfortably. Her shoulder grazed his calf as she tossed one boot aside. In her fumbling, if Sestra's head grazed his erection, he'd jump out of his skin. He looked down, her body the lodestone drawing his attention. Sestra bent forward, a sensual, a white hourglass kneeling at his feet, her waist nipping small above rounded hips wiggling sweetly as she unlaced her garter.

Knees locked, his fingers dug into her clothes. Otherwise, he'd bend over and grab her soft white bottom with both hands and not let go.

She covered herself with hudfat again and stood up. "You're next," she said with too much cheer.

Was she affected at all?

He walked around her to a low branch. Jaw set, he hung up her clothes with his leather bag and stowed his weapons inside the shelter. She turned away when he removed boots and clothes, but he was careful to stay facing her.

Darkness couldn't hide everything.

Cool air saturated his skin, calming his loins and clearing his brain. He wore nothing save the iron amulet, the metal warm on his breastbone instilled courage to deny himself. He'd denied himself much for years, and this was one measly night.

With her back to him, Sestra waited at the mouth of the shelter, his sleeping fur wrapped around her. So quiet, too quiet. She was fatigued, but this was inner turmoil. She didn't toss out saucy comments. She waited to see what he'd do.

He scrubbed his face both hands, lack of sleep blurring his vision. His body screamed for rest, yet he couldn't ignore Sestra's skittishness. She expected him to pounce from behind. Why wouldn't she? Telling her he'd tear off her clothes and make her go naked back to Uppsala destroyed what trust they'd built.

"Sestra." He gentled his voice and touched the hudfat. "I have to take this."

She nodded meekly as he gripped the fur at her nape. His fingers brushed smooth skin and curls fine as a babe's hair. A tiny moan came from her, the sound a feather-soft caress to his insides. He hesitated. Coddling wasn't in his nature, but the little noises she made threatened to undo him, made him want to sweep her into his arms and plant tender kisses on her lips.

Hugging herself, Sestra's gaze slanted at him over her shoulder, her profile pale against midnight trees. "Take it."

The fur fell away. Round, creamy curves showed like smoothly carved ivory in darkness. Her bottom's cleft was a slender black thread on white flesh. He itched to run his finger down the enticing line. How soft would her skin be there?

He grasped her shoulder. She was shaking.

"I'm cold."

Her small voice shook him to the core. "Don't be afraid," he murmured. "We sleep together, sharing the fur. For warmth."

Pine needles crackled in the silence as she turned. Chin up, she faced him, one arm crossed over her breasts, the other shielding her most vulnerable feminine flesh. The saucy mouth he craved was set, a thin line of damning silence, but Sestra's turbulent eyes pierced his heart sharper than any knife.

Years of having no say over herself reflected back to him.

Her brown eyes seared him. He had to look away. "I won't...use you."

Naked in the forest tired yet wanting, his body desired Sestra. His lusty cock bounced stiffly at the sight of her. For all his harsh history, he wanted this woman of all women to have a little faith in him; he was no rutting animal. He'd gone too far in pushing her away and now there was little he could do but live with the damage done.

Body wracked with tension, he stretched the long fur bag inside the shelter. He pulled open the flap and slipped inside the hudfat on his back, but he made the mistake of raising his head to call Sestra.

Head up, his tongue refused to work. Faint light touched the fiery tuft of hair between her legs. She stood in profile at the shelter's entrance, her body visible from the waist down.

"Are you ready?" she asked.

He fixed on the patch of red hair. "Yes." The word strangled his throat.

Sestra dropped to the ground and crept toward him on hands and knees, white hips undulating, ripe breasts swaying creamy and large. He ogled her, devouring every inch of freckled skin. Her nipples peaked with tender points barely visible in the shadows. Imagination filled in what he couldn't see.

Head flopping down, his erection tented the fur. Hot rigid need was taking over. How badly he craved easing the ache between her legs. A few strokes of her hand in the right place and he'd spend his seed. The image of Sestra's alluring body burned itself on his ragged brain and wouldn't let go.

Staring at rough wood overhead, he dredged up quelling memories.

Swimming in icy water. Hunting muskox. Fish guts. Falling in a swine's pen. Rotten hen's eggs.

Sestra tucked herself into the hudfat, her bare legs slipping along his. He froze, sucking in a sharp breath and shut his eyes. A foot lay flush to his calf. Sestra squirmed alongside him, and the curls between her legs skimmed his hip. The sweet fiery tuft of feminine hair…

Eyes shut didn't help. His mind worked harder, picturing what he couldn't see.

Palms driving into the ground, he exhaled raggedly and squinted at the shelter's handiwork. Sestra nestled against him, adjusting the hudfat. She dragged the fur this way and that over his pulsing erection, the coarse fur giving bittersweet friction on sensitive places.

"Stop moving," he ground out. Breasts squished him, the softest pillows on his chest and ribs.

"I'm getting comfortable. Trying to," she mumbled, her breath fanning his nipple. "Your sleeping fur is too small."

His nipple puckered. "Because it's made for one." The ragged words coming out his mouth hardly sounded like him.

Night wind roused the island's trees. Stars winked at him between cracks where the branches leaned together. Surely Freyja watched from above, finding great delight in the Frankish thrall sprawling naked across his body. Denial already turned his balls into painful stones.

The need to feel, to give in to his body's demands consumed him.

Swimming in icy water. Hunting muskox. Fish guts. Falling in a swine's pen. Rotten hen's eggs. Rancid milk. Putrid meat.

Sestra wriggled her cold body on his. "You never finished telling me what men do when they cheat death."

"What?" His head lifted off the ground. "You know the answer."

Her dark eyes sparkled with mischief. The little shrug she gave was torture, rubbing her heavy breast along his rib. "I do, but I'd feel better if you talked to me."

Her voice was intimate on his skin. He swallowed hard and willed his mind not to think about lush curves pressed close or fiery red feminine curls snug against his hip. Or the sweet freckle at the side of her mouth.

"Go to sleep."

Wiggling, she made her little humming noise. "This won't work. The opening here, it's cold on my back." Her leg swung across his thighs. "I want to sleep on the other side."

He groaned and shut his eyes. "Just get comfortable."

Darkness magnified every wriggle, smell, and sound. Sestra's knees buffeted his thighs as she straddled his waist, the whisper of her skin caressing his new torture. The tendrils of her woman's hair brushed him intimately. Was it possible he felt each strand feathering his aching cock? Cool, clean air carried scents of pine and pitch, filling his nose and biting his nipples.

Two hands rested on his chest. "Is this how you like sex when you cheat death?"

His eyes shot open. Sestra straddled him. The center of her palms pressed his nipples. Feminine legs folded against his hips and thighs. His hands curled easily around firm calves and wouldn't let go.

Her hand trailed down his body's midline, sending waves of bliss across his skin. "Never mind," she said archly. "I decided this is how *I* like sex after I've cheated death."

Sestra's hand moved to the dark spot between her legs and his. She teased the black hair between his legs before her fingernails delicately scratching his abdomen and going lower. Shivers danced across his thighs. A drop of his seed glistened on the tip of his cock.

Air hissed past his teeth. "Sestra…"

"Today was a first for me." Her fingers found his dampness and swirled it over the crest of his manhood. "I learned a lot hanging onto that root." She paused to squeeze his rigid length, her feminine laugh throaty.

His heels dug into the fur. Her hand was exquisite.

She started stroking him again. "It changed me."

"You don't...have to do this." Hips jerking into her, his body sung a different tune.

"Oh, but I want to," she purred.

He wanted badly to be gentle with her, but it wasn't his nature. He liked sex the way he lived, fast and rough with no time for a lover's gentle words. If Sestra only knew the beast caged within, she'd not want this. If she yielded to him, he'd ride her hard and slake this animal thirst.

Fingers gripping her calves dug deeper. She'd have bruises tomorrow because of him, marks on her soul because of what he'd said and marks on her body because of what he'd do. His heart twisted in his chest. She deserved better than this.

"If you don't stop now, I can't stop..." The words burst out of him with a curse when she seated herself on his cock's rounded head.

"I don't want to stop."

Pleasure-pain centered on her hot, wet skin kissing the crown of his erection. Sestra sat tall over him as if he was conquered and she the victor. With the tiniest shift, she gave needful friction. Her legs were firmly muscled under his hands, the skin soft as silk. She drove him out of his mind, rolling her hips in slow, sensuous circles. Slick flesh teased no more than a single inch of him. All sensations centered on the tip of his cock.

117

"Sestra," he growled.

Eyes innocent, her hips swirled wide. He almost slipped out. His head jerked up. Stomach muscles knotted. Sinews strained.

He *had* to stay inside her.

"You've never touched me," she whispered, one hand on his chest, pushing him down. "Never even tried to."

His body shook from fighting unquenched need with all his might. He. Had. To. Push.

"Gaahhhh." The roar ripped from him.

He grabbed her hips. Her thighs were the best of strong and soft in his hands. Grinding with all his might, he thrust into her like the beast he was. Her breasts jostled. Air skipped sharp and fast from her mouth. The artful hip circles stopped.

Flesh slapped flesh.

Quick. Desperate. Pressure built in him with each cry slipping from her lips.

"Ohhhh," she cried long, her head lolling sideways.

He grabbed her breasts. She whimpered, arching her back. Erect nipples the size of rose hips squashed against his palms. He grunted and squeezed the supple breasts filling his hands, the down-soft skin pale against his claiming grasp. He wasn't gentle.

"Brandr." His name was an exhale on her lips.

This was animal need. A hot race.

Sestra shifted slick intimate flesh against his. The angle pressed him high inside her and she cried out, a high, keening pitch. He slammed his hips into Sestra, her feminine wetness making snicking sounds the faster and harder he pushed. Her slender, sinuous neck stretched long. Starlight framed the riot of curls fallen free.

Sif... fertile, beautiful, life giving.

Sestra's beauty overwhelmed him, matched only by the storm of want from pushing into her. She set her hands over his on her hips and moaned her pleasure.

Each primal sound she made captured his heart.

"Shirin-am." His throat hoarse, the foreign words wrenched free. *"Eshgh-am."*

His muscles tensed from head to toe. Head and shoulders lifted off the fur. He'd bite her if he could. Craving roiled in a hot ball, shooting through him. He rammed into her. Hard. Fast.

One...more...thrust...

A roar ripped from his throat.

His cock pulsated inside Sestra. He grabbed her braid and she fell onto him, the tight sheath of her body milking him, an intimate kiss from her most secret place. He shuddered once. Shuddered again.

Fulfilled. Sated. Wide open to Sestra.

His hands roamed her back, her hips, the side curves of her breasts. Soothing hands calmed her and the beast inside him. Eyes closed, whispered words spilled from him. He was half-aware, floating in between this world and his pleasured state.

Sestra unseated herself and slumped over to the enclosed side of the hudfat. Nestled against him, her breath tickled his chest. She stroked his breast bone and rested her hand there, his amulet of Tyr under her palm.

A slice of cold air touched the other side of his body. He smiled, a sated wild creature, glad to bear the open side of the sleeping fur for Sestra. Her rose hip nipple pressed his rib while the other poked out from the fur. Sestra's big breasts drove him out of his mind. Smiling with utter contentment, he pulled the fur up, hiding the pink-red fruit. He could never let Sestra know how much he loved her breasts and her big brown eyes. Or her tantalizing freckles. It'd be too much power. The saucy redhead would easily lead him by the nose.

Tender lips pressed his jaw with a gentle kiss. "My thanks. For today. I'll never regret this time on the island with you."

His heart turned to a lump of clay. He'd guess she didn't want their togetherness to end. Neither did he.

"You're welcome."

She settled her head under his chin. "You saved my life, and you've been mostly nice."

Nice? He mouthed the word in the dark. The trait wasn't natural or unnatural, simply unknown. He lived a brutal life. Sestra's voice, honest and humored, chipped away at deep walled-up places.

He knew Sestra, the thrall who served ale. Sestra, the flame-haired tease warriors sought for a tussle. Tart-tongued Sestra who met him in a battle of words, but what else did he know?

Flesh against flesh, she molded her body to his. "You're right. Two bodies together heat up fast."

Quiet laughter gathered in his chest. "After what we did, yes." He kissed the top of her head, finding comfort in their tangled limbs.

He'd never lain this way with a woman, two naked bodies twined together for the night. Stroking her spine, bone-deep contentment covered him, swept from chest to limbs, spreading like a potion. Staring at the wood poles slanted imperfectly together, knowledge hit him hard. One day alone with Sestra was all it took. *He knew.*

He loved her.

All summer he'd fought the saucy redhead's unexplainable draw. Curt jabs and a surly tone were useless weapons against her appeal.

"You're a good man," she sighed nearly surrendered to sleep. "You deserve good fortune building your ships on Gotland."

Gotland.

He flinched. Sestra had stood before him bare-skinned and fearless tonight. She gave him her trust, the one thing he didn't deserve. Outside the shelter, he'd swear two ravens perched on the log facing the shelter's opening. Wind stirred the leaves, whispering Odin's truth: *There are few tokens of ill than a man not knowing how to accept the good.*

Of his choices, did he know which one was for the good?

Eyes growing heavy, his fingertips drew meandering circles on her back. He slowed on the crest of her bottom and settled his hand on a curve he'd swear was formed for him. He knew how to fight, how to scout, and how to build boats. He knew what to do with a woman's body.

What was he going to do with Sestra's trust?

Chapter Eight

Brandr was gone.

She sat up fast, the fur dropping from her shoulders. Island air needled bare flesh as sunshine poured through cracks overhead. The Viking wasn't near. She sensed the loss of his presence the same as she smelled him on her skin. He'd marked her soul. Shifting her hips, a twinge nipped tender skin between her legs. She threw back the fur.

Her warrior scout marked her secret places too.

She rose gingerly and scooted out of the shelter. The forest floor chilled her feet. Birds warbled sweet morning songs. Her russet tunic and white underdress hung from the same low branch as last night, but the spot beside them was conspicuously empty. Brandr's weapons and bag were missing too.

His vow...he'd not abandon her.

Shivering, she yanked the linen underdress off the tree and tugged it over her head. She snatched her tunic to her chest and bent low for her boots and the small knife, when her ear caught a sound.

Whistling. From the beach.

Tunic and boots clasped to her bosom, she trod a careful, bare foot path following the music. When she came to the edge of the grass, her heart lurched.

A perfect male form rose from the water.

Brandr. Of course he didn't desert her. He stood waist-deep in the channel, his big hands rubbing sand everywhere.

She ducked behind a tree and breathed a prayer. "Bless the Vikings for their need of cleanliness."

Sand made a natural cleanser for tables and cooking pots. Why not enticing male?

She could go back to the shelter. Wait for him. But water splashed, and his whistling—a strange sound from the surly warrior—begged for another peek.

Did last night's hearty swiving put him in a good mood? She nibbled her lower lip. No highborn woman with silk sheets gave him satisfaction. She did.

Brandr rinsed himself, and her mouth went dry. Morning light glinted on a hundred water beads meandering down his body. She'd take her time, too, if she were a droplet. With full sun this morning, each water spot shined like a diamond stuck to his torso. Ink black hair sprinkled his chest. A natural crease split his torso down the middle, separating muscle born of hard labor and hard fighting. She followed the furrow to its end in water and pressed full-bodied against the tree.

A nasty, apple-sized bruise flared red and purple on his waist. She covered her mouth. Yesterday, the Viking's hammer had struck him. Plenty of scars marked his chest and arms, tell-tale signs of his brutal, warrior's life. A big white scar slashed his ribs. Another thick one snaked over his shoulder. And she wanted to explore each one in daylight.

Rough tree bark abraded her tender nipples and bit her cheek. The thin underdress rubbed bothered skin, places she wished he'd touch…softer with his fingers. Last night was a rush. She'd straddled him, yet Brandr rutted hard, feverish and desperate. Her thighs pressed together at the memory.

The Viking scout liked sex the way he lived—rough.

Finding Brandr in the simple act of washing himself was intimate, as flummoxing as his unexpected kiss last night followed by cruel, confusing threats to promising not touch her. He could have taken her anytime this summer. It was the way of things with thralls.

What went on between them was…different until last night, when *she* made a bold advance.

A kiss was one thing, straddling a man, well, that was entirely another. She smiled and her hand slid between her legs. Through linen, her fingers rubbed damp heat as Brandr dunked in the channel. She could tip-toe back to the camp, and he wouldn't be the wiser for her gawking.

He emerged, wading toward the beach. She made herself small behind the tree. Hair slicked back, Brandr wiped his eyes, the water swishing around him. Carved hips gave way to powerful, sinuous thighs. Between his legs, black hair and his—

"Morning, Sestra," he drawled.

She knocked her forehead against the tree trunk, heat creeping up her face. This was so wrong to be caught like a maiden taking her first peek at a man.

Brandr pulled his trousers off a rock. "Did you sleep well?"

She sighed. "Very well. And you?" she called back, her nose on the bark.

"Better than I have in a long time thanks to you."

Skin tingling everywhere she inched out from behind the tree. He grinned and put one leg in his trousers, facing her in all his male glory. Brandr wasn't in a hurry to get dressed.

"Pagan Northmen," she scoffed under her breath.

"What's that?"

"Nothing."

Nor did she like how in command he was, how utterly undisturbed at being naked out in the open. She strolled across the beach, her gait stiff. It was pure feminine pride, but she wanted him to be more affected by last night. She certainly was with heavy breasts and craving between her legs. Whistling was a good sign, but she wanted him to pounce on her. Sore or not, she wanted to pounce on him.

She stopped a hands breadth from him, her clothes a barrier. Brandr calmly belted his trousers, the sun shining on his wet chest. The iron amulet of Tyr dangled in the hollow at the end of his breastbone. Tiny grains of sand clustered on black hair encircling his nipples.

One confident finger swiped a brown nib with the barest touch. "You missed a spot."

Brandr's nipple shrunk and silvery eyes slanted at her.

She gloated through the veil of her lashes and kept up her delicate assault, tracing the black hair around his nipple. Arms at his sides, Brandr's chin dropped to his chest. His eyes glinted hot and dark, following her finger. She let her clothes drop.

On the side of his torso, her nails raked the angled trenches his ribs and muscles made. She traced a pale scar and reveled at his body expanding and contracting with hoarse breaths under her touch. Spine straight, her fingers skimmed his midline to his navel. This was what she craved…this sense of power.

He grabbed her hands. "Sestra."

A storm brewed in Brandr's tarnished eyes. She loved the way he said her name, his voice thick with need. Were other parts of him thickening?

"This—" He kissed her hands folded in his. "—we can't."

"You mean last night was a better time? Exhausted as we were fumbling in your sleeping fur? A squirrel's nest has more room."

He laughed, the deep rumble caressing her insides. "The fur is made for one."

"You should do something about that."

"You weren't too bothered last night."

She averted her eyes. No. Last night she rode him like a horse.

"This morning I'll make up for it," he said, resting her hands against his chest.

Standing this close, her heart fluttered. This close in daylight she marveled at the colors of his whiskers. Jet black hair covered his square jaw sprinkled with auburns and browns. His smile widened enough to crinkle the corners of his eyes. His vague promise barely registered from the joy writ on his face. Happiness came in short supply for Brandr.

How good it was to bask in this moment. Rugged, yet, perfect. Like him.

How could she have thought him too hard?

"Pray tell."

His gaze landed on her collarbone. "You have dried blood here. From the knife tip at your neck," he said gruffly, and traced the bone with one finger. "I should've taken better care of you."

"It's nothing. You vanquished two men and saved my life. Just another day for you."

Brandr ignored her quip and brushed back curls loosened from her braid. "What's this?"

His thumb caressed the ridged scar curving around her neck. Few ever noticed it. She didn't pull away, a baffling thing since the mark embarrassed her.

"From days past in the land of the Franks."

"What happened?"

Droplets sparkled on his shoulder. He smelled of water and earth, the effect warming her better than the sun. The channel lapped the beach behind him. Birds flew overhead. The people of Uppsala strove to throw off the yoke of war, yet alone on this island with Brandr, they could be an ocean away from the tumult.

"I was required to wear an iron collar to keep me from running away."

He scowled at the scar. "You never told me about this."

"It's not something I talk about." She tried to smile, but his thumb stroked feather-light touches. "Now you know there was a time I desperately wanted my freedom. Mostly to escape the cruelty."

127

"When you were a young girl."

She nodded, her eyelids heavy. This piece of her past, a truth shared, freed her. Her head lolled sideways, all the better for his hand to explore her neck. "It was after my mother died. I was sold to a Frankish farmer. I wanted to run away. To stay near the place she died. I never thought beyond fleeing my circumstances."

"What happened?"

A cold shiver, shade from the past, passed over her. "I paid a high price."

Brandr kissed the scar with a caring, gentle peck.

"Now I want freedom the right way...to purchase it and decide my own path." She tried to breathe but air came in fits and stops. His lips caressed the scar line, brushing back and forth. The soft tease melted her inside, healing soul-deep damage.

Could a man's kisses blot out a lifetime of pain?

Hidden places on her body waxed hot. She leaned into him, her legs not willing to hold her up. Brandr's mouth warmed her with lingering kisses, grazing the slope of her shoulder, hovering a hair's breadth from her skin as if her nearness was enough. His mouth was in no hurry to reach hers. Both his hands skimmed the length of her back, landing on the high curve of her bottom. Big hands palmed her, abrading linen over tender skin.

She pushed up on tip-toe, her hands exploring his chest where his heart beat hard against her palm. Ticklish whiskers scraped the high curve of her breast, and she laughed with delight frothy as sea foam. Brandr's warm mouth traveled higher, his breath hot on her flesh.

128

Her hands slid into his wet hair, discovering those soft curls at his nape. She sighed sweetly and cupped the back of his head, drawing him closer. Brandr nibbled the corner of her mouth and she shuddered all the way to her toes.

"Ohhh." Her knees buckled, but he caught her by the waist.

The surly Viking tasted her as if she were a sweet morsel. Safe in his arms, her head tipped back and her body yielded to his strength. Dark light flashed in his eyes. If Brandr was a beast of the forest, he'd drag her to his lair and never let her go. This must be a glimpse of the warrior who spent much time alone in wild lands.

"Please," she whispered, rubbing her mons over his erection. "Kiss me on the mouth."

His lips molded to hers for one long, deep kiss, soft yet hard like the man. Her heart soared. Legs tangling, her body rocked against his. If the beach was beneath her feet, she couldn't feel sand anymore.

She was free.

Strong hands gripped her shoulders and pushed her away. Brandr said a foreign word under his breath, a curse word by the way he nearly spat it and let her go. Her sluggish eyelids opened halfway. His hair, shiny and black, fell around his jaw.

Iron-colored eyes burned. "No. We can't."

"No, we can't what? Kiss? Lay naked together in your sleeping fur?"

What was behind his need to deny fleshly pleasures?

As if he read the question in her eyes, his mouth flattened grimly. "Remember why we're here."

Eyes narrowing, she couldn't shake his vague answer. A few stolen kisses couldn't hurt. Yet...the damaged boat. The dead men from the clearing. The treasure and the people of Uppsala.

"You're concerned about the other warrior," she said, willing her heart to slow down. "The one you think will come back."

"He *will* come back. Rats always do." He lifted his tunic off the rock. "I won't be caught with my trousers down. We need to get moving."

"To Lord Hakan's farm and give him the news." But her lethargic limbs refused to cooperate.

Metal clanked as he strapped on *Jormungand*. "You'll want to put your clothes on."

Stomach rumbling, she shook out her tunic. Bright saffron and blue threads fluttered, the embroidery torn when Brandr saved her from the cliff. Every moment with him thrilled her, challenged her ordinary life of servitude. So many possibilities with him...

This couldn't be the end?

She smiled and raised her tunic over her head. "You make me feel safe," she said quietly. "I forget there's trouble on the other shore."

Questions tumbled through her mind. What did the foreign words he whispered last night mean? Why kiss her passionately and push her away as if she was poison? He *was* right. They needed to get off the island. Niggling doubts hung over her head, but a new plume of black smoke rose in the distance. Her questions could wait until he was a captive listener on their boat.

The tunic dropped over her face, the russet wool veiling her eyes and sliding over her nose. When she tugged it all the way down, Brandr waited in front of her, a long knife balanced in one hand.

"I'll need to cut off your hem."

"My hem? Why?"

"To repair the boat." He eyed her skirt as if deciding how much to cut. "Wool strips soaked with resin seal the planks."

Glossy saffron and blue embroidery shined on the dark wool. The threads, she suspected, were silk. No thrall wore silken threads, but it was hers to keep. With careful tending, the mud stains could be cleaned and the rips repaired with artful stitching.

"Couldn't you cut my linen underskirt instead?" Her heels inched backward. "I've never had clothes this fine."

He stopped surveilling her hem to look in her eyes. The corners of his mouth softened. "Wool holds resin better."

Her shoulders sunk. *What else would the island demand she give?*

She took stock in the healer's forest across the water, a stiff breeze blowing curls loose from her sleep-mussed braid. Hadn't she sacrificed enough? The treasure was lost. She was hungry, and more men like the one who held the knife to her throat were coming. Brandr was only thinking of their survival. It's how he lived.

He flipped his blade around in his hand and went down on one knee. Without a word, he began to untie his boot's leather cross garter.

"What are you doing?" she asked.

The leather garter dropped in the sand and Brandr, head bent to his task, pushed down his boot. "Preparing to cut my trouser leg off."

"What? No! Stop." She skidded on her knees and grabbed his hand with the knife poised to cut.

The depth in his grey eyes took her breath away. Wind teased Brandr's ragged overlong curl at the side of his neck and she wanted to melt. Firm male lips curled in the kindest of smiles, erasing harsh lines that framed his mouth.

"You would go with one leg clothed just to save my hem?"

She could barely swallow. No man had ever smiled at her like this...as if her whim was his command.

Brandr hooked a finger under her chin. "I would do much more to see you happy."

It's be easy to fall in love with him. To love his square, stubborn jaw and proud nose with its bump in the middle. He'd likely broken it once and reset it himself. Brandr, she discovered was as ruggedly beautiful on the outside as he was remote and beautiful inside. The woman who cracked open his private heart would find a treasure worth hoarding.

"No. You can't," she whispered, her mouth dry.

"Can't what? See you have some happiness?"

His graveled voice caressed the deepest places inside. Tears threatened to come at the man she wanted but couldn't have. She belonged to someone else, and Brandr couldn't afford to buy her.

She pushed his knife aside and retied his boot. The small act lightened her. "I thank you for your concern, but my hem is a small price to pay."

His brows pinched at the words *price to pay.*

"You're certain?"

She stood up, steeling herself for the first rip. "Cut away."

Brandr's knife jabbed a hole in the hem, and her body turned in a slow circle to the music of rending fabric. One rotation complete, and the bottom section of her tunic was gone. Walking to the pine tree, Brandr notched the wool with his knife and shred it into smaller strips. He stretched the cloth over the tree's oozing lines and pressed. When he removed his hand, resin darkened the cloth.

Daylight poured over the tree's scored lines. "With full sun here, we won't have long to wait." He glanced up at her. "Heat makes the tree bleed faster."

She turned to the sun, its warmth blasting her face. Last night, he'd cut in the exact spot where morning light would shine the longest. He read the elements, sun and sky, moon and stars, water and land.

"You've done this many times, haven't you?" she murmured, lost in the quiet.

Wind rippled tiny waves across the channel. Pine needles crunched behind her. Brandr stood close enough the heat of his body touched her.

"A few. You're the brave one here, a giving woman."

"I'm not so sure. We're returning empty-handed."

The ebb and flow of his steady breath was as intimate as last night's sex. This newness was to be savored. True comfort with a man who made her body burn and her soul sing. How long would it last? Her gaze slid to the ripped wool bathed in sunlight. For as long as it took the tree to yield enough of its blood. Everything paid a price. The boat would get them off the island, but it would also take Brandr away.

He stroked her braid as his lips moved over her ear. "If you could choose freedom today, would you take it?"

She whipped around. "Are you asking me to run away with you?"

Chapter Nine

"You claimed the treasure was lost," she said, hiking her skirts above her knees. "Today you think you'll find it?"

"There's a chance," Brandr called back. His long legs ate up the island path, leaving fern fronds swinging in his wake.

"But you were so sure."

Water slapped the shoreline ahead. Brandr jogged to the break in the trees. When his booted feet hit the sand, he never lost his stride. Nor did he respond as he veered to the right across the beach. Near the mouth of the stream, he set his leather bag on a rock and pulled out balled cloth. Linen corners fell away, revealing dried apple rings and part of a barley loaf.

"Eat. Your stomach hasn't stopped rumbling." He broke off a piece of bread. "I'm sure it's why you're asking foolish questions."

"You mean about running away with you?" Holding hair off her face, she took three dried apple pieces. "Or the wisdom of coming back here?"

"Both," he said wryly before he took a bite.

"I'm trying to understand. Last night, you were so convinced the treasure was gone." She nibbled on the dried fruit, its sour-sweetness exploding on her tongue. A quick swallow and she finished, "And why wouldn't I think you meant running away? You've talked about my freedom more in one day than I have in all my life."

"Running away is foolish."

His teeth ripped off another bite of bread. Wind blew black hair across his jaw as he chewed. The elements were stronger on this side of the island, the wind harsher, the sun sharper, the water rougher. Brandr slipped warm fingers along the side of her neck. He stroked the ridged scar hidden in her hairline, his black brows arching.

The mark of her slave collar when she ran away years ago.

"But you'd protect me."

"For how long? Once Uppsala's turmoil ends, Sven Henrikkson would hunt you down. Is that how you want to live? Always looking over your shoulder?"

"It was a thought," she said weakly.

"Not a smart one." His thumb teased her ear lobe, softening the insult. "Better to gain your freedom."

A spangle of pleasure trailed down her neck from the tiny bit of flesh he stroked. Brandr might prefer to rut like a hardened beast, but his tender touches were sweet bread crumbs, leading a woman to abandon herself in his lair. His kisses devastated her the way his mouth hovered over her lips as if her breath alone sustained him.

"And if I buy my freedom, I go with you?" she whispered.

"You can't." He turned abruptly and stalked off to the stream's edge.

Brandr stood wide-legged, his broad back as forbidding as the scowl etched on his profile. He ate his bread in silence, the water dribbling over the toes of his boots. Food lost its flavor as she chewed. This was his way...an insult, a rare show of heart-aching tenderness, and this. Silence. Or she suspected disappearing altogether such as he did at Lithsablot.

She'd have better luck finding the silver coins today than wrenching words from the Viking scout.

Beyond the shore, a seagull dove at the open water. Wings flapping fast, the bird's claws dipped below the surface. A battle of perseverance went on between the bird and an unseen creature, and the seagull swooped down on the other side of the shallow stream facing Brandr, a squirming fish its reward. The gull's yellow beak tore into fish flesh, its small eyes on Brandr. The bird dared to squawk at him until other seagulls invaded the feast.

The Viking lobbed his crust and the winged interlopers dashed for the morsel. "Enjoy your prize while you can," he said to the bird devouring the fish.

Brandr ranged across the sand, his head bent in deep thought. This sudden remoteness was a cold blanket. It was a mistake to boldly ask pointed question to a private man. She'd pushed him more than drew him out. Deeper questions about his purpose in coming here would simmer unanswered.

He took three mint leaves from a small leather pouch, and stuffed them in his mouth. Without a word, he offered two leaves to her on his outstretched hand.

She accepted the gift and put them to her nose, inhaling the freshness. "How are we going to do this?"

"We wade upstream. See if we can recover anything from the water." Brandr put his things back in the modest leather bag. "We need to get a palm's for you and another palm for those who've suffered."

Her gaze shot to the water. He said *we*. Nor did he speak of getting a palm for himself. "Yesterday you couldn't wait to get out of there. The treasure didn't seem worthwhile to you."

"Because it was dark and your safety was more important," he said knotting the leather ties.

She broke off a piece of dried apple, nodding sagely. "Ah, your vow to Lord Hakan."

The food could be leather in her mouth. Niggling doubts about his explanation ate at her, but like all lies, what he said held a ring of truth. She couldn't dispute him.

Brandr worked around her, stiff-shouldered, not looking her in the eye. Wind stirred soft black curls on his nape. After last night, she could claim knowledge of another soft part of him—his lips. How was it the same mouth that taunted without mercy could cover her with the finest kisses?

Facing the upstream, he spoke over his shoulder, "I didn't think the smaller hoard was worth it."

"But today it is."

He turned around, his silver eyes pinning her. "Today it is."

"You're doing this for me."

"I want you to have your freedom."

No finer words had a man ever said. Gorm, the coming berserkers, even the good people of Uppsala she hoped to help, all paled. Her life, her wants, mattered to Brandr. His warrior's sense would have them stay by the boat, but he risked all for one more attempt to get the treasure—the much diminished treasure and *her* best chance at freedom.

But why his sudden coldness? That among other questions sprang to mind.

"You didn't buy me, did you?" she asked quietly

"No. I don't know who did, but this gives you the chance to claim your future." One hand fisted at his side. "No running away."

Her shoulders rounded forward. Well, that settled that. He'd already slammed the door on a possible future. By the aching touches he gave, she had an inkling he harbored some feelings for her, but not enough to reach beyond the island. Yet, he cared plenty to try again for the treasure. It meant both of them going into the water if Brandr had his way. After yesterday's attack, he wouldn't leave her on the open beach while he hunted for the remains of the treasure.

She walked to the stream where it fanned out on the sand. Her heart banged as she followed the water line into the island. "What about the boat?"

"I'll fix it as fast as possible."

Her skirts swayed, the tattered hem's russet threads trailing over her pale underdress. "The man you said would return. Didn't you say he'd come back with others?" She frowned at him. "We'll be outnumbered."

"It's a gamble I'm willing to take," he said dryly.

Of course he wasn't bothered. Yesterday, he'd killed two men when she'd been more hindrance than help.

"Not very promising considering your luck with gambling."

Brandr tensed visibly at the jab. She squashed a sand clod with the toe of her boot. They'd hardly stopped kissing and were already back to old habits.

"We can watch wool soak up resin if you like," he said with all patience. "Or we can give the treasure one last try."

"What remains of it in all that...*water*." She couldn't help but shiver.

Brandr rambled over to her, the wind teasing his black hair. Sunlight bounced off his sword hilt. This could be the same as any other day for him, risking life and limb without a second thought.

"You sung a different tune last night. You weren't going to let water or darkness stop you." He gave the sun a split-second look. "At least now we have daylight."

She squinted upstream, her breath thinning. "Last night was different."

"You mean your warrior's elation."

"I felt unstoppable." Today she landed with a thud.

"At heart you're a fighter. You'll face your fears. With me." Brandr's gruff voice lulled her, appealing in its roughness. He grabbed her hand and gave it a squeeze. "We'll walk together. As far as you can, but I need to keep you in my sights."

Saffron threads from her torn skirt whipped around his legs. Mist billowed in the distance where the waterfall crashed.

"That's about knee-high for me."

"Then you know how far you'll go." He paused before adding, "It's only water."

Broad shoulders blocked out the sun's glare. Holding Brandr's hand, they were in this together. The fierce Viking had a way of knocking her fears down to size.

"Why is it with you, I feel like I can do anything?"

A bright smile creased the corners of his eyes. "Because you can."

Taking a deep breath, she nodded. "Let's go."

With late morning sun beating overhead, he led her into the stream. Behind her, waves crashed. Before her, water flowed. Beside her, Brandr walked, holding her hand.

Her heart lodged in her throat from willingly striding deeper into the stream. Gurgling water sped past her ankles and soon inched its way up her calf the more they hiked upstream. Cliffs began to rise on either side of them. Silty sand gave way to smooth stones. Rocks jumbled, and each step she took was cautious, her foot testing the rounded stones.

"You know," she said, bracing a hand on a large rock, "I would think your Odin is making this journey especially difficult for us."

"The lowest fence is the easiest to cross."

"More of Odin's wisdom?" She stumbled on a wobbly rock but strong arms steadied her.

Water nosed its way around her knees.

"You'll value your freedom more because you're fighting hard for it." Brandr's long legs sliced through the rushing stream, sure-footed and constant.

A few more careful steps and icy water crept up mid-thigh. A fine vapor welcomed them. Smooth river rocks carpeted the crystal clear stream, making steps easier. When she raised her head, the dead Viking's body bobbled in the waterfall's pool ahead.

She glanced over her shoulder, the beach small and distant. "One night, we'll sit by a fire, and you can share all your Viking lessons with me."

It was small talk, something said to soothe herself, but Brandr stiffened. Mist coated his face. Without a word, he stopped and started to unbuckle his sword. He'd grown distant again. Was this his warrior's focus? The same as when he navigated the channels to find their way here?

A vexing idea struck her: he demanded she face challenges with courage, yet Brandr kept to his safe world of stoic silence.

Where was the bravery in that?

She teetered on the awkward edge of knowing the man intimately, yet not knowing him at all. The Viking's remote character she understood, but his strange push and pull drove her mad. The island was becoming a place of reckoning. Last night she fought for her life on the cliff. By daylight, she'd fight for the truth. It was hers to claim.

Her wayward mouth blurted, "Why is my freedom so important to you?"

Chapter Ten

Brandr's fingers slackened on the buckle. Head bent, his gaze rose to hers. "You don't want your freedom?"

"I do," she insisted. "Yet, I question why you've pushed for it more than I have." She eyed the dead Viking, his body pummeled by the waterfall. "Actually, I've a good many questions."

"Such as."

Water beaded on Sestra's cheeks and spiked her cinnamon lashes. She raised a shaky hand and swiped wet curls off her forehead. She'd faced her fear and gone deeper and farther in the water than he'd expected. Pride made him want to believe he had a hand in that, but she deserved the honor. By her direct stare, Sestra's courage came with the brash need to dig into places he'd rather keep buried.

"What did you say to me last night? Those foreign words when you were inside me? What do they mean?" She rattled off her questions, her arms spreading in supplication. "And why the change this morning? We kiss and all of a sudden you push me away? I vow you're more inconstant than a skittish virgin."

"You ask a lot of questions."

"And you're short on answers," she said tersely.

Water skipped over rocks, its cheery gurgle a contrast to the drenched, angry woman standing before him thigh-deep in the stream. He finished unclasping the buckle and let the leather straps hang loose.

"You really want to know *now*?" he asked, hands on his hips.

"Yes. Now." She smirked. "It's only water."

He balked at having his words tossed back at him. Glaring at her wasn't working. Despite the water, Sestra upraised chin told him no way would she back down. For her courage alone he wanted to kiss her.

"Go ahead. By my count, you've got one left."

Her brown eyes rounded. "The fearless Viking hides behind his game of three questions," she said, head shaking slowly. "No wonder you're alone."

High cliffs shadowed Sestra. Root tendrils sprouted from the cliff behind her, a reminder of yesterday, and her brave bid for life. Much had passed between them on this unfulfilled quest. By her firm tone, she meant to lash out at him, but the jab barely nicked the hard wall he kept around his heart. He was alone by design until a certain flame-haired thrall got under his skin this summer.

If she could face her fear of water, he could face down a single, probing question.

Body tensing, he braced for the blow. "Your one question...what is it?"

Her mouth rounded. "Is talking to me so awful?"

He hesitated. Talking wasn't bad, as long as they never shared words of depth or spoke of the future. Both were things he couldn't give.

Seconds passed, measured by fiery emotions flickering in her eyes. "I was mistaken. You owe me nothing." She pivoted fast, clutching sodden skirts and pushing into rushing water speeding past her hips.

"Sestra, stop!" He lunged for her and grabbed her shoulders. "Do you have a death wish?"

The falls drummed. Wraiths of swirling mist danced across the pool. Her reckless march brought them steps away from a steep drop. The pool darkened to the deepest blues where the stream bed plummeted.

"Keep your treasured secrets," she said, trying to wrench free. "I don't need them and I don't need you."

He flinched. The tip of her red braid floated in the stream between them, a lifeline he wanted to hold fast and not let go. His nature was neither kind nor open, but he brought her to this, led and coaxed and prodded her along as if her freedom was his. The stony wall inside him crumbled. He should've kept her in safer, knee-deep water.

No. He should've hied off for Gotland instead of vowing to watch over her. Sestra needed a better man than him.

"Ask me anything," he said, hands firm on her shoulders. "I'm not letting go until you do."

Shadows swarmed overhead from a hundred ravens darkening the sky. Her back to the cliff, he sat her on a round boulder. Sestra's mist-dampened face tipped high. Gone was the saucy thrall, replaced by a bold maid with a mouth he wanted to devour. She stared at him as if she would out-wait him. In the game of patience, he could tarry long past the first frost if she wanted. His flame-haired temptress had no idea what she bargained for.

Sestra's life vein bounced against freckled skin at the base of her throat. The throbbing slowed until her shoulders eased.

"Why is my freedom so important to you?"

Her even voice asked the same question she'd asked moments ago, one he'd ignored.

"I don't know."

"Give me something better than that," she said, her brown eyes flashing. "You owe me the truth."

His lips clamped at the much-deserved challenge. Ravens roosted on the cliff. Their beady yellow-black stares were all-seeing and all-knowing. Of all the questions she could've asked, this one tested him dearly.

He stepped back, holding her gaze. His thumbs hooked the dangling leather straps and *Jormungand* slid free.

"Hold this." He laid his sword safe in its leather hilt in the crook of her arms.

"What are you doing?"

"You'll see." Grasping handfuls of his tunic, he pulled the black wool from his body and turned, giving her full view of his back.

She inhaled sharply. Muscles knotting in the cold, he stared at bright blue skies, ready for the worst. It'd been a long time since he'd seen his back reflected on polished silver and longer still since another laid eyes on him there. Water splashed behind him. Sestra's toes banged his heels, and her breath fanned his bare skin.

"What is this?" Her hands skimmed above his right shoulder blade. "Are they letters?"

"A tattoo. In Persian," he said, keeping his voice level. "It says I am a *bahadur*, a fighter who belongs to Hassan ibn Dawla."

She gasped. "A slave?"

His vision hazed on the cliff wall. "For most of my life."

Flesh pebbled under her curious hand. He shuddered, held captive by waves of pleasure flowing over skin hungry for touch. Sestra's fingers traced a spot numbed from burns near his shoulder. She needed to touch, to learn, and read him. He understood this. His back told tales far better than words, yet her gentle discovery was carnal agony.

Eyes shuttered, unfathomable humiliation washed over him. Thralls were a way of life for Vikings, but male slaves were of the bottom order. Some masters valued them, others deigned them the lowest kind, unworthy of respect. He'd kept the despised secret long buried.

Sestra's fingertips explored the dark lettering. Each light caress connecting him to a dark and evil time. Where she touched, he'd lost much feeling. Burns marked the tattoo, his frustrated effort to blot history. He opened his eyes and scowled at stones underfoot. Time and persistent water smoothed the river rocks, giving them their shape. Part of him still fought the truth of what he was. He couldn't take back the past and mold it into what he wanted it to be.

Perhaps he wasn't as wise as he thought. Nor were his rough edges smooth.

He never let people see his back. When women tried to remove his tunic, he'd divert them with pleasure. If they persisted, he'd pull away, speaking rudely or abruptly leaving their beds. The women who sought him for bed sport begged for coarse sex, a thing he was happy to oblige.

Sestra traced long scars twisting along his spine. The lashes. The last sign of his old life.

"I thought you were Viking," she said.

"I am. Born of a Viking mother and father in Trondheim." Skin hot, he tucked his tunic under his arm and splashed his face. The icy water felt good. "My father died in a raid when I was a babe." He turned around, giving full attention to unraveling his tunic. "My mother hated the sight of me...it was my earliest memory."

"Did she beat you?"

"No," he said, laughing harshly. "She sold me instead."

Sestra's brown eyes glistened with tears.

"Don't pity me." He slid both arms into his tunic. "I was better off. Sold to Egil, a Viking shipbuilder of Estland."

"It's not pity."

His ire fed him, made him charge headlong into the tale. "There were two things Egil loved most. Building ships and his wife, Grete. When I came along, both treated me like a son. I lacked for nothing showered in their love."

He hesitated at the word love passing his lips. The admission oddly stripped him as much as it made his spine straighten. He had been loved. He was capable of giving and receiving love.

"Why did you leave?"

"It wasn't by choice." He jerked the tunic over his head. "I was big and newly bearded when Egil and I went with others to trade in the south. A storm hit, knocked us off course. I washed ashore on the Abbasid Caliphate. Slave traders found me and took me to Sousse."

"And Egil?"

Metal bands could be crushing his ribs from the pain of spilling his past. His whole body ached. The blurred past flashed before his eyes. Egil holding onto splintered wood, waves crashing over his hoary head. The old man fought hard to survive, but one of the waves swallowed Egil. The Viking never surfaced.

He swallowed hard. "Lost at sea."

"Boats and water. They steal everything good." Sestra's pale, freckled hand touched his wrist, curving over his leather arm brace.

"Your reasoning needs much work." A grin formed a split-second before faltering. "Boats aren't bad."

"I know." Her chin dipped. She squeezed his arm and let go to hug *Jormungand* tightly to her chest.

"Like you, water has been at the crux of my misery."

Standing in cold water, he felt nothing. Not the stones underfoot. Not the hunger from meager provisions. He stared at the rushing falls, looking but not seeing. His own body drifted feather-like into a dream world above and to view himself and Sestra.

"What happened at Sousse?" she asked softly.

He wanted to answer her, but his throat refused to work. *Sousse*...the booming seaport with its scorching sand roads had blistered his bare feet and was the beginning of stealing him body and soul. Her question probed the deepest, tenderest part of his wounds.

Overheard serrated raven caws cut the silence.

Did Odin demand he give his due of truth and revelation to a slave woman?

Shirin-am. Eshgh-am.

Persian words for an Odin-bestowed gift. Sestra. The scheming All-Father favored courage over status. Men and women could be slaves or kings, Odin didn't care. It was their boldness and cunning that counted.

Sestra. His head tipped to azure skies above. He'd swear a breeze blew her name into the ravine. The earthen wall she'd climbed last night bore signs of her struggle. Claw marks striped the dirt above the broken root where she'd fought for her life. He'd fought for his life more than once, living the outward battle to survive.

His hand settled over his heart where fresh pain threatened to crack him like an egg. In a strange way, he was fighting for his life on this island.

"Sousse was the beginning of my misery," he began, his voice hoarse. "It's where Ibn Dawla bought me. My size and black hair suited his needs."

"For...for..." she covered her mouth, her eyes rounding with horror.

He fathomed her meaning. Slave markets bustled with men buying women to sate baser needs. Few men met such a fate.

"No. Ibn Dawla preferred women, had a harem full at his fortress on the Tigris River."

The Tigris, *The Fast One*, the people called her, yet a poor man's shallow vessel could navigate her well. Standing in the island's stream pulled him back to the days of wading in the Tigris.

"I lived near the river far north of Baghdad. Trained in stealth, scouting, and fighting; a weapon the general used in rising tensions between Persian and Seljuk Turks."

"I've heard of this Baghdad."

"A place teeming with people, more than the sands of the sea."

He could see the aged beggars, their sad lined faces and outstretched hands. Bodies packed streets where small children scurried in and out of narrow alleys taught to steal before they lost their first tooth.

"You hated it." Sestra grasped his forearm with both hands, her face tipped high to his.

"Hot, dry, no real forests such as we have here."

Filled with a thousand scheming men and women who never touched a weapon, yet they cut down swaths of innocents in their hunger for wealth and power, using skilled fighting men like him.

"You yearned to be free."

Harsh laughter rattled him. "More than you can ever imagine. I was desperate for the Northlands. Thought of them every day."

"You're here now." Sestra's voice was softer than silk.

Her touch sought to drag him back from the dark place, but he was lost. Long suppressed memories demanded their due. He couldn't stop this tide. His lashes masked his eyes. If Sestra tried to see him, she'd see a dead man.

"Ten years I did his bidding. The general's favorite. I learned Persian and Arabic, spoke it like it was my mother tongue." He stared at the water rushing past, lost in those vivid final days...

Swords clanked in the fight yard. Sheets of sweat poured over his skin. Oppressive heat bore down enough to send horse flies to the shade. He knocked the newest bahadur *on his back, sending up throat-clogging dust clouds.*

"Uhhh," the man groaned, his body curling in a tight ball.

Brandr nudged him with his foot. "Get up, Armenian."

A bahadur was stripped of his name, called only by his birthplace.

"Viking." The general's voice cracked loud across the yard. "Come."

His bronze-headed mace landed with a thud on the ground. A slave boy scurried forward and snatched the club. No one approached the general with a weapon. Men grunted around him locked in battle. None ceased fighting as his leather-soled sandals sunk deep in soft sand on his walk to the general. Every new moon the overseer had fresh sand brought to the yard to strengthen men's legs.

He stood before ibn Dawla's shaded canopy in a blood and dirt-stained loin cloth...a prized animal.

"Sit." The general waved his hand at a red silk pillow. He dipped a morsel of lamb in murri, the brown sauce the old man favored.

Brandr's mouth watered at the tangy aroma. A feast of baked fish, bowls of rice, grapes, and lentil stew all filled brightly colored dishes on a red-embroidered table cloth. The old man often ate cross-legged at his low table while watching the men practice their battle skills.

Feet rooted to the ground, Brandr tore his attention off the food.

Ibn Dawla's shrewd eyes narrowed. "You're hungry, but you never accept food at my table."

"I eat when the others eat."

"Yet, you partake of my harem when I throw open the lattice doors." A crusty laugh floated across the table. "You're a stubborn one."

"What do you want?"

The old man pointed a bony finger. "Don't be rude." He paused when a housemaid set an ampoule of wine on the table and two silver chalices. Her black gaze flickered Brandr's way before she poured the wine.

"I give you too many freedoms, Viking. Too many. But you are my best fighter." Ibn Dawla sighed and raised his full chalice. "You can have a day in your treasured mountains if..."

A day to roam the spring green mountains near Kirkuk, the spoils of a job well-done. Better than a night in the harem. The general only bestowed the reward of a day in the mountains after he accomplished the toughest tasks.

A dozen soldiers would camp in the valley below while he breathed cool mountain air, and the same men would take him back in chains the next morning.

The general talked, and he nodded without listening. This would be his time. This would be his escape.

Brandr met Sestra's questioning gaze. "I ran away and it nearly killed me."

"That's why you want me to buy my freedom."

There was more. The wish for her not to be satisfied with enslavement, the wish for her to fight for what else could be hers. The wish...

He scowled, facing the waterfall. "The Henrikkson's won't do to you what ibn Dawla did to me when I was caught running, but if you ran away, you'd forever be looking over your shoulder."

Her hand slid up his body and settled over his heart. "What did he do to you?"

"Beat me. Badly. Before I passed through Hel's door, the general sold me. I went to the Balearic Islands and served a Moorish pirate...as a galley slave."

Sestra covered her mouth. "Oh, Brandr."

He was glad she didn't spout meaningless words. Nothing could soothe this agony. A galley slave's life was nothing and worth less than nothing.

Wrists tethered to their seats, galley slaves rarely left the cramped, low-ceilinged hold. Men rowed day and night, eating, sleeping, heeding bodily needs through a hole in the bench. The wood stank of piss and death. Overseers cracked whips on all bare backs if one man slumped in exhaustion. Overseers cracked whips if they thought a slave wasn't working hard enough. Overseers cracked whips for the cruel joy of destroying defeated men.

Insolent to the core, his stubborn defiance nearly cost him his life.

He didn't have to give more to Sestra. He'd wrapped his vicious animal past into the tightest coil and let it fester in deep places, but tender brown eyes read him well. She grasped his roaring pain and dared to unravel it. The ruthless

154

beast stirred inside him, unwinding within, lured by the flame-haired *Sif*.

His mouth twitched at Sestra's talent for loosening his tongue. "One day I heard grapple hooks, men shouting. Our ship was attacked. The overseer came below and cut free all the slaves." His voice cracked. "Except for me."

"You were left to die?"

Wet curls stuck to Sestra's quivering bottom lip. He brushed them away, finding solace in the small act. Above her more ravens gathered on the ridge. Wings flapping, the birds lunged and pecked at each other, jostling for a place on the cliff. Bits of dirt and grass fell in the stream behind Sestra. Air nipped his lungs. His body wracked with agony in this telling, but jaw set, he'd finish this.

He turned his right forearm over and began to untie his arm brace. "The overseer wanted me to die with my hands tied to the sinking ship. I yelled for help. Tried to free myself." His breath came in gusts. "I yanked hard enough the leather straps tore my skin."

The brace slackened, showing the white scars. His teeth grinded. "I *hate* having my hands bound."

"How did you get out?"

"Hakan." Chin tipped high, his body relived the sinking ship, the screams of men dying, the choppy sea water creeping up his neck, and splashing his mouth. He'd swear he could taste the ocean's brine on his tongue.

"He heard me cursing Odin and came below." Gulping air, he blinked at blue skies, yet all he could see was the hold's low ceiling. "Water came up to my mouth. I jammed my cheek against the ceiling for air."

"That's when Hakan came."

155

He nodded slowly. "I saw his blond head dive under water. He cut me free and dragged me back to his ship."

Dead men had floated in stewing seas. The Moor's round-hulled galley ship sunk before his eyes, its lateen sail swamped by waves as strong hands hauled him onto Hakan's Dragon ship. He collapsed, vomiting sea water wearing nothing more than a tattered loin cloth. Viking warriors gathered around, their Norse music to his ears. Thunder cracked—*Did Thor rage at his cursing Odin?*—and men parted for Hakan the Tall. Rain pelted the chieftain's head as he waved off the warriors.

"And Hakan brought you to Uppsala."

"Yes," he said, laughing without humor. "To be his slave."

Chapter Eleven

Sestra almost dropped his sword. "You're a *slave?*"

"Not anymore. This past year I served Hakan by choice as House Karl."

"A freeman," she said, needing the certainty of the word.

"Yes. Freed last summer." Eyes downcast, he tightened his arm brace. "After saving my life, he suggested I serve him seven years or swim to land."

"But you were in the middle of the sea," she said her voice notching higher.

Brandr chuckled coldly. "Hakan can be very…persuasive."

His face clouded as he tugged the brace's leather thong. Arm folded across his midsection, his other hand fumbled with the tie. It was his way. Live alone, work alone. Shadows engulfed them despite the bright sun outside the ravine. They could be sinking deeper into the earth. The island's waterfall tumbled its deafening noise, but Brandr's pain roared loudest in her ears.

She set his word on a rock and touched his hand. "Let me."

A black lock fell forward, grazing his whiskered jaw. Brooding eyes searched her under hooded lids. Brandr let her take his hand, and he watched her intently like a beast allowing a humble creature to care for his paw. Long slabs of muscle framed the warrior scout, gave him power to prowl wild places with ease, but his heart proved fragile.

A woeful ache yawned inside her as she wedged his forearm under her breasts. Uppsala could burn for all it mattered. Brandr deserved tender care, a lifetime of it, if she had her way. The stream swirled around her hips as she tied the leather strings. The task done, she couldn't let go. His arm was solid against her, the same arm that had lifted her off the cliff and built the shelter that covered her last night.

She opened Brandr's curled fist and kissed his palm. A minty fragrance clung to his thumb and forefinger. She sucked lightly on one and then the other.

He inhaled sharply above her head. "Sestra."

His ragged voice lulled her. Brandr's black brows pressed together, agony writ all over his face.

She cupped his cheek, gently brushing back the errant lock. "I will never forget this time on the island with you."

Black lashes shuttered his eyes. The treasure, freedom, hers and Brandr's, all braided together here. It was a mystery she couldn't divine nor would she try. Ravens flew overhead, too many to count. In her side vision, the dead Viking bobbled in the pool, most of his body yielding to his watery grave.

"I regret my harsh insults this past summer." She paused and gave him a half-smile. "Well, not all of them."

He laid a hand over hers on his cheek. "Most were richly deserved. I am a bad gambler."

"One year as a freeman…that's why you have little wealth."

"Thralls don't share in the spoils." He grinned at her. "Hakan tried to give me some, but I refused. My seven years weren't done."

"Stubborn man," she said under her breath.

He kissed her caressing hand. "I prefer to call it determination."

"And don't forget prideful," she added, her thighs pressing his under water.

"It's confidence." He cosseted her hand between his.

"You always lived with the other House Karls."

"It was Hakan's decision. None objected when my bahadur skills saved their lives. Fight hard, show courage, men will respect you."

"The Viking way," she snorted.

"The way of a good man," he corrected.

"I can think of other things that make a man good," she said fiercely. "A good, kind heart for one."

His smile hinted at tolerance, the kind one gave a spoiled child who had yet to learn the ways of the world. Her cold legs hurt, but she had so many questions and Brandr was tender-eyed and open.

Her gaze slid to *Jormungand* resting on the rock. "What about your sword? Surely Hakan didn't give it to you. Even I know it's costly."

"I didn't steal it. It was paid for with all the wealth from my first year of freedom."

Her knees wobbled. "And you were going to give it to, to him—" Chin slanting at the dead warrior, her voice was contrite, "—to save me."

"To save you."

Her mouth opened but no words came. A man who had little was willing to sacrifice the one costly thing he owned to save her. He valued her that much?

"You're getting cold." Brandr's thumb brushed her lower lip. "Why don't we see what we can find of the treasure and get off this island?"

And now he was going to risk himself to recover as much of the treasure as possible. This wasn't about saving Uppsala. This was about saving her.

She nodded numbly. "Yes." To wanting this brusque warrior to warm her, to gaining her freedom, to a future with him.

His lazy smile spread in black whiskers. "Wait here."

Shivers started up her legs. Standing in cold water took its toll, but truth would not be stopped. It cropped up at the most unexpected times, as solid as the man slicing upstream.

Water crept higher up his broad back until only his head was visible. At the pool, Brandr dove underwater near the jagged rocks. The dead Viking's body, mostly underwater, floated to the middle of the pool. The falls thundered. Ravens swooped off the cliff, their wings flapping an awful noise in the ravine. Two birds shot up to a high pine tree edging the waterfall. The rest flew downstream, a black trail against the vibrant blue sky.

She picked up *Jormungand* and hugged the sword against her chest. Her lips began to quiver from standing so long in the stream.

Where was he? How long could the Viking stay underwater?

"Brandr," she yelled, a useless thing since he couldn't hear her, yet she called again louder, "Brandr?" Her voice echoed off the ravine.

This was foolish. Even if he needed saving, she couldn't help him. But she could try. Grabbing hold of a boulder, she stretched one leg forward. He was underwater too long. Her other leg shook before finding firm ground on a rock.

"Brandr." This close the waterfall drowned out her voice.

His head poked up from the water and he swiped water from his eyes. "I don't have it."

"Bran—"

He ducked under again, his boots frothing up the pool. Water rippled outward in a wide circle, and the dead Viking's body drifted downstream. She took two more steps forward and planted a steadying hand on another boulder. Neck stretched, she peered at darker water. Water bubbled up where he had to be deep under the surface.

A hard object tapped her elbow.

She hissed, slamming into a rock. The dead man's booted foot bumped her. His cloak snagged on large stones on the other side of the stream.

"Ewww." Grimacing, she nudged his foot away with the tip of Brandr's sword.

Brandr shot up from the pool, his fist raised with the torn leather bag. "I have some of the treasure," he shouted. "I can get more."

"Wait." Her cry was in vain. He set the bag on a flat boulder and dove under again.

Silver coins winked from the bag. Was this freedom?

Water dripped from her lashes as she followed the dead man's body veering downstream, feet first. His cloak wrapped around the rock like discarded laundry, holding him in place.

Would she be ready to move on?

Ripples circled wide across the pool's surface. A woman's face reflected back, red tendrils stuck to damp skin and large brown eyes the color of river rocks below. The stones were hard, but she was soft and knowing and better off for coming here. She'd stood up to the Viking warriors in Lady Mardred's longhouse. They didn't deserve her help, but she gave it, the same as letting the treasure go.

These were acts of will. Her will. The wish to live and thrive blossomed strong, and the first thing to do was release a dead man.

"I can do it." She sucked in a deep breath, repeating firmly, "I *can*."

Her hands trembled with cold, rattling Jormungand against her. She dare not use it. If she dropped his prized possession and it fell into the pool...

"You have a knife of your own," she reasoned through chattering teeth.

She'd need to learn to defend herself. Viking women settled for nothing less.

She set *Jormungand* on a dry boulder and set her foot on a rock. Reaching down, she grabbed her knife handle tucked into her boot. Loose saffron threads drifted in the water from her bodice. The sharp blade came free, and she held it up to the blue sky. This is what happens when courage demanded action.

The pair of ravens watching from the pine tree cawed as if giving their approval. Wading across the stream, she ignored the bloated Viking and his pasty skin. Her small blade sliced easily through brown wool. The cloth gave and the dead man floated downstream, taking her fears with him.

She wouldn't live in the shadow of death.

Behind her, Brandr broke the surface again, both hands pumping the air. "We did it," he called out, his smile bright white in black whiskers. Fistfuls of silver shards and bronze arms rings shined in his hands.

Raising both arms in victory, her laughter echoed in the chasm. "No, *you* did it."

Brandr dumped the treasure in the bag, the water roiling around his body as his legs churned under the surface. He clutched the bag in one hand and swam toward her

When Brandr stood safely on the river rocks, she tucked the knife away. "Now we can get out of the water."

He wrapped an arm around her waist and twirled her in the stream. "Now you can be free."

Full of glee, they trudged hard, the water pushing their backs, driving them, she hoped, to be together on Gotland. One question stood in the way.

Who had bought her?

Chapter Twelve

"My eyes are brown like dirt. You know, no one sings the praises of dirt." Sestra stepped from the tub near the open shutter, and snatched her plain linen underdress to her skin.

Night fell soft and black outside Lord Hakan's longhouse. Crickets chirped evening songs, a reminder nature carried on despite the battles of men. The farmstead was eerily empty save the massive eiderdown bed. Tables, benches and chairs, chests, soapstone lamps, dishes, weapons—all traces of life—were gone.

When Lord Hakan's man was missing, Brandr decreed they'd wait.

The former bahadur rose silent and shirtless from stoking the roaring fire pit, orange and yellow lights dance across his skin. The corners of his mouth curled, his tolerant smile, the one he used when listening to her prattle.

Happiness flared inside her at his doing simple chores with his back exposed. He trusted her.

"And freckles," she sighed, hugging her stained underdress against damp breasts. "Poets don't wax on about those either."

The fire outlined his long, powerful legs covered in oft-mended wool trousers. Brandr's bare feet, long and beautifully arched, stepped quiet as a cat across the earthen floor.

Her heels inched backward the more he advanced on her. "I'm simply saying brown eyes are nothing to sing about."

One glimpse at the bed and her limbs turned rusty. Lying with Brandr was much more than two bodies rubbing together. The island changed that. Questions tumbled in her mind. Once free, where would she go? How much longer would Brandr watch over her? And the most pressing of all, would he promise to have sex with her alone for the rest of their lives? Simple questions really.

Her bottom hit the wooden wall. "In Frankia, many women have brown eyes. They—"

Brandr touched her lips with one finger, the smell of river water on his skin. Black hair fell loose around his freshly shaved jaw gleaming smooth and kissable.

"Your eyes are the color of earth. Without it we don't eat and trees can't grow," he said. "We'd have no place to stand unless you prefer rocks. I don't. I'll take fertile and brown. It's the softest place to land for a man like me."

She gulped. His rough voice gentled her all the way to her toes.

Tiny flames danced in Brandr's eyes. "You're nervous again."

"Uh-huh," she nodded, tasting salt on his finger.

He braced a hand on the wall beside her head. "Why?"

Her gaze went to two leather bags on the floor. One, Brandr's belongings. The other, the paltry remains of the treasure hoard he'd found in the pool. She'd cut off excess leather and retied the bag. As soon as Lord Hakan's man showed, they'd take their palm and Brandr would go his way, and she would go to hers. The old silver coins and dented bronze pieces didn't shine so brightly anymore.

A lump built high in her chest. Had been there since they left the island. Her arm holding the linen against her body squeezed hard. "I want to go with you."

"To bed? You can't miss it. It's the biggest thing in the longhouse."

She giggled. "It's the *only* thing in the longhouse."

Brandr had dragged the massive bed closer to the fire pit for warmth. While she bathed, he'd sat on the eiderdown bed to unlace his sleeping fur. Task completed, he snapped the heavy fur over the bed the way washer women snapped fresh linens.

The Viking made comfort out of starkness. He'd repaired their boat and rowed them back to Lord Hakan's farm. When no one was there to greet them, he roamed about the lonely longhouse, cleaning up broken pottery shards and building a fire. He soon trapped two rabbits and cooked a stew with pearls of barley and wild onions in the remains of a large broken cauldron split in two.

When she'd grumbled about her dirtiness, he unearthed a coopered tub from the barn with gaps between its slats. As the sun slipped low in the sky, Brandr heated water in the other half of the broken cauldron and tightened the tub's iron bands, producing a fine bath. She soaked in hot water, and he cleaned himself in the river. She was done with rivers and streams for a while.

His lids drooped lower. "I've already been inside you. Why so unsettled?" He brushed wet curls off her shoulder.

Too many men had used her. Men had said worse, yet her cheeks warmed at his bluntness. "I'll thank you to remember this is different." Air hiccupped in her lungs. "We're different."

The back of his hand skimmed her shoulder. "Last time, I was rough." His voice dropped to a near-whisper and he kissed skin he'd just caressed. "Tonight will be different, *shirin-am*...I promise."

Her skin prickled on his deep-timbered *promise*. This wasn't about one night. She wanted all of his nights.

His breath smelled of mint, the leaves he must have chewed because he knew he'd kiss her. They barely touched yet her limbs grew heavy. Brandr traced a lazy line down her arm to her waist. His calloused palm slipped behind her. She jumped when four fingers slid into her bottom's cleft.

Her head lolled sideways on the wall. "*Sheeran-am*? What does it mean?"

The linen undergarment abraded tender nipples, slipping lower from its purpose to drape her. Brandr kissed one faded freckle after another on her shoulder. She was powerless to insist on conversation as he whispered foreign words against her skin.

Brandr rooted out a lock from hair falling down her back and pulled it over her shoulder. "Persian for *my sweet*."

He concentrated on the red coil, his thumb and forefinger straightening the curl all the way to its tip. Firelight caught rare gold strands. His curious touch could be the wick showering sparks all over her body. A pulse teased soft skin between her legs, and the flesh folds felt heavy.

Still, she had to know.

"Do you promise to lay only with me for the rest of your life?"

The curl sprang free. "You're unsure of your future."

"Yes. Especially with you."

Brandr's lids dropped low. Both hands traced arcs across the tops of her breasts. The round curves brimmed over loose cloth she was about to drop. Her arms were heavy and her nipples begged to be touched. Wetness trickled between her legs. She fidgeted, pressing her thighs together, the pressure adding to her misery.

He scowled at his fingers caressing her. "I'm not the best man for you."

A small line slanted between his brows. If she read him right, the Viking didn't like how much he craved her breasts. His nostrils flared, and his mouth opened as if he'd devour those curves and not stop.

"That's not the answer I'd hoped for," she said weakly.

A shadow passed over Brandr's face. "I want to be, but I'm not."

The Viking cupped her high, freckled curves with both hands. Gentle and seeking. She trembled. Her toes pressed hard into the earthen floor. The fierce bahadur battled against his own needs and wants. She covered his hands with hers, seeking connection. She found Brandr's textures—rough skin, the roped scars born of desperation reaching from his wrist, the play of muscles and sinew on strong, life-saving hands.

Beyond the open shutters, a breeze blew through untended rye fields. The Fyris River beside the fields, the river that would take him away.

"Don't pull away from me." His voice was ragged with need. The heels of his hands teased her nipples through the linen with the barest pressure.

The excited tips poked hard against cloth. Her body knew what it wanted— his hands rubbing her skin, his hardness inside her, a connection deep enough to forget where she ended and he began. The future was tomorrow. On the island, she'd untangled his last tortured secret.

Tonight, she'd let the man unravel her.

Bending close, his mouth hovered over hers. "*Doost-et daaram,*" he whispered. "*Doost-et daaram.*"

His kiss was tenderness and life. Brandr coaxed her with small kisses, each touch of his lips a word he couldn't say, soul-stripping kisses gentle enough to make her body sway and her legs part.

His lips delighted in the side of her mouth. The warrior mumbled something about a freckle. His hand released its grip on her bottom to slide on her belly under the linen she clutched. One tug and he ripped the cloth barrier away. Brandr stepped back, his eyes taking in her feet, her knees and thighs, halting on the thatch of hair between her legs.

A shuddery inhale reminded her to breath.

Ridged stomach muscles clenched as if in pain. Eyes glazed darkly, he reached out and cupped her mound. "You are *Sif.*"

The pressure of his hot hand could make a woman forget her name. Her shoulder blades scraped the wall from the need to rock into him. Did he feel wetness gathering in her hidden folds?

"If I'm *Sif*, you're hard as rock," she teased, cupping him back.

He braced a hand on the wall again, the tendons cording his forearm. Shaggy black curls fell around his neck. Brandr's head dipped and the dimple in his cheek appeared.

The big, bad bahadur was clay in her hands.

Brandr stared at the freckles between her breasts, the muscles in his jawline twitching. The gold and silver of all the Viking kingdoms couldn't buy this moment. Brandr's simple touches, light kisses, his smoldering stare.

Let men conquer for shiny pieces of metal. Women seized the better treasure.

Her hand slid deeper between his legs, finding his balls. Air hissed through his open mouth. The more she kneaded him, the harder his stomach muscles knotted. Brandr's arms and chest tensed hard enough to shake.

This had to be the beast she met in the shelter. Hungry. Desperate. Rough.

His head swooped between her breasts and he licked a freckle on her cleavage. Brandr kissed the spot, sucking and muffling words about tasting her freckles. The growling moans on her breastbone shot liquid heat inside her, down her navel, past her abdomen to the fragile lips between her legs.

170

Big, calloused hands clasped her breasts, squeezing her nipples, rolling dark pink flesh. Mouth open, his brow darkened. The pliant nipples fascinated him.

"Come." Her hand hooked inside his waistband.

"What?" Brandr glared at her, his mind snared in lust-filled fog. The indent etched deeper over his nose.

Leading him by the waistband, she took him to the edge of the bed. The fire cast its molten glow across the sleeping fur. Darkness pitched all around the longhouse save where they stood. Shadows flickered across his jaw and a wicked smile spread.

Tiny flames burned in Brandr's silvery eyes. "I'm forgetting the finer points of seduction with you."

She loosened his trousers' leather ties. The backs of her hand bumped his flat belly, and two fine rows of taut muscle tensed above Brandr's navel. Orange light contrasted with the deep purple bruise on his waist. He'd lived a hard life. Now she'd soften his path all the rest of her days.

Her breath raced. "You don't have to with me."

He liked rough sex. She sensed it, even if he wouldn't fully admit aloud how powerful the want was. Nor did she give him a chance to say so when she kissed him full on the mouth, open, her tongue brushing his, sucking the tip, mimicking on his tongue the rutting he'd do to her. The kisses were wild, wet, and unashamed of fleshly pleasures.

Brandr's big hands grabbed her bottom, squeezing her plump seat. Their bodies rammed together. Friction. Bumping. Her thatch of hair grinding hardness in his wool trousers.

He cupped the back of her head and broke their hot kiss. Panting, he rested his forehead on hers. "We're going too fast."

She pushed his trousers down and the black wool slid to his knees. "We're not going fast enough."

Brandr's erection bounced on her belly. Waves of gooseflesh swept over his thighs, his chest, and arms. She fondled the length of him as one might stroke a pet, playing with the long, smooth hardness. "This would be a bad time for Lord Hakan's man to come for the treasure."

Brandr grabbed a handful of her hair at her nape. "Sestra," he growled.

His heavy breath came in fits, yet his hot forehead stayed touching hers. He needed her as much as she needed him. She loved him and she lusted for him. The desire for Brandr burned in every fiber of her body. Her nipples ached, her skin tingled, and she wanted him inside her. This hot craving for Brandr left a mark far deeper than bodies against bodies.

Love wasn't a language she fully understood, the taut connection that made one man and one woman want to be together forever. She knew one thing. He filled her.

And, she smiled wantonly, now he was going to fill her.

"Here." She pushed him back and settled her bottom on the edge of the bed. Spreading her legs wide, she let him take his fill of the little red bush that fascinated him.

A tendon stood on his neck. Her feminine outer lips parted and cool air caressed hot flesh. She braced herself on one elbow, her other hand sliding through slippery skin, stirring wetness. Rubbing, massaging, provoking. Enough to make Brandr's life vein throb above his collarbone.

Hot, wanting pressure tormented her. The cradle of her hips tilted forward, pushed back, tilted forward, and pushed back.

She bit her lower lip, stifling a moan.

Brandr towered over her, his glazed stare locked onto her circling fingers. Little snicking noises sounded in the deserted longhouse. The bed ropes creaked.

"This is what you want," she said, stroking springy curls between her legs. "For the rest of our lives."

She thrust her breasts high, unashamed at her ploy to lure him. She wanted him for all the right reasons. When he grabbed himself and slid his erection into her, she wanted him for all the wrong reasons, too.

His large, sun-bronzed hands rested on her pale thighs. Brandr crashed into her, stopping to wonder at black curls mixed with red.

"Look at that." His voice was hoarse, and the iron amulet around his neck swung wildly between them

Orange firelight played over the slopes of his shoulders. His nipples were tight brown circles on his chest, the center nub a tiny point. Brandr began to slide out of her, all the way to his tip.

She whimpered and nudged her bottom forward.

Brandr stopped when the crown was barely inside her and he waited. She licked her lips and scooted closer, the sleeping fur rustling on eiderdown beneath her. He grabbed her bottom cheeks, halting her.

"Lay back." A lazy smile spread over his face. "I have control *eshgh-am*."

She sunk back on the downy mattress. Her mouth opened to ask the meaning of the foreign words, but Brandr grabbed himself, angling the tip, touching the sensitive spot high   inside   her. Quick. Short. Thrusts. Pleasure flared everywhere, embers sparkling under her skin. Her body bowed off the bed. The sweet pressure…fullness right where his fullness touched.

This was why a woman's body existed. To float on a cloud of pure ecstasy. To let a man gift himself to her and know the purest of connections.

Her bottom quivered on the fur beneath her. Hairy male thighs rubbed her inner thighs. Bed ropes creaked harder. Black hair fell around Brandr's face, his silver eyes intense. He bent over her and bracing a hand beside her hip, his other slipped between them.

She jolted from white hot pleasure.

His finger joined the tip of his cock.

"Gahhh," she cried, her body bowing higher the more the rhythm flowed in and out.

Her eyes widened. She clutched the fur. Shock and bliss centered on the strange touch between her legs. The tip of his finger and his hardness brushed lightly inside her.

She writhed, yanking fistfuls of fur. "Brandrrr…"

"Let it come *eshgh-am*. Let it come." And he bent forward, grazing her nipple between his teeth.

Angling her head, she glimpsed his hand aligned with his cock, palm facing her, moving in time with his hips. Slow. The way he rowed, back and forth with measured strokes, making each one count. His control like his strokes turned her limbs to melting butter.

"Brandr." She gulped air. "I'm…it's…"

174

Never again would she look at oars and boats with dislike.

The bed creaked, louder and faster. Noise came from her, grunts from Brandr pumping harder between her legs. The beast he tried hard to hide unfurled.

"I can't...." He removed his finger and lunged fully into her. Hard. Fast. Rough.

Brandr braced his hands on either side of her waist. His hot forehead rested on her chest, new sweat glistening on his shoulders. The Viking grunted with every thrust. The bed shook like stormy seas. He rammed into her, and she rammed back with all her might.

Darkness covered her eyes. Wetness dripped over her tender folds.

The beast of need took over her body. She grabbed the hair on Brandr's head with both hands, shoving shameless hips into him. His teeth grazed her other nipple. Shudders exploded across her navel.

"Brandr...you are so, so..." Her words were lost.

Thoughts fluxed to nothing. She couldn't talk. She wouldn't try.

Her body was reduced to pure, fluid feeling.

Through her lashes, she watched him. Hips pounding, Brandr suckled her nipple before opening wider to take more of her breast into his mouth. He devoured her, sucking a mouthful of the freckled curves. Her jaw dropped. She couldn't swallow. Brandr took half her breast into his mouth all while his hips drove her stunned, pleasured body into the squeaky mattress.

His animal stare met hers, glowing and predatory in firelight.

And with a popping sound, his mouth released her breast.

Jiggling, freckled skin glistened. Her fleshy nipple poked high for more. He inched up her body and his tongue laved the dark pink skin. Eyes smoldering, his hot mouth hovered over her other breast. Sweat trickled down his forearm. His rutting hardly slowed. Growling against her skin, Brandr kept eye contact as he covered the pliant inner curve with his mouth and bit.

Pleasure-pain spiked hard. He left his mark. Faint indents on pale freckles.

Tremors shook her thighs. Wild animals bit when they mated. His claiming bite rattled her. Her body sheened with sweat, bowing high and hard, slamming into Brandr's chest before her back dropped onto the bed again. She buried her face in the sleeping fur, her final cry hoarse.

The Viking slammed one final time, roaring against her breast. Stars spangled bright against the dark wood rafters before all went black.

Chapter Thirteen

Soft cloth brushed her thighs. "Wake up."

Thick eiderdown dipped from Brandr's body seated by hers.

Tangy smells of heavenly sex mingled with earthly smoke. Sestra squinted at sharp daylight. The longhouse door and every shutter had been thrown open.

Brandr caressed her hip. "You'll want to put your clothes on."

Sitting up, she wiped her eyes. Her tangled hair tickled her back. Air touched her skin everywhere save the pile of clothes in her lap. Her boots sat at the end of the bed. She grabbed those first.

"I must tend to my needs," she said slipping on her boots.

She hastily gartered the boots and ran out into blinding sunshine to take care of her body's needs behind a line of trees beside the longhouse. The yard was empty save the broken cauldron. Rye stalks bowed under a breeze blowing off the Fyris River.

Finger combing her hair, she strolled naked into the longhouse. Passing through the lintel, she announced, "I see why Vikings are unbothered with showing their bodies." Light laughter bubbled up. "It's freeing."

Brandr leaned by an open shutter. "If you're not careful, you'll give Lord Hakan's men a free display of your charms."

Hips swaying, she strolled to the bed. His grey eyes burned, following her the way cats traced birds. She hitched a foot on the bed and retied her boots.

"We go from Persian words of love to this cool greeting. You're a fickle one, Viking." She made sure to give him full view of every freckle.

A muscle ticked on his jaw. "We need to be ready."

She took her time tying her other boot, but her efforts were for naught. Brandr turned away, surveying the forest and river. Sighing, she yanked her underdress on fast. She wanted to tempt her grey-eyed bahadur, not get caught naked by other men. She pulled on her tunic and sat on the bed. The gentle creak must've been too much. Brandr's head swiveled around fast, his features tense until his gaze caught her fully dressed.

"Is our readiness your only concern?" She separated three sections of hair. "Or is something else bothering you?"

He checked outside the shutter where birds flew past before giving her his full attention. Arms crossed tightly, his hands rested on his ribs with both thumbs on his biceps.

Her stomach rumbled. "Please tell me we get to eat first."

"I'll check the traps in a moment."

Neck prickling, she forgot the braid and hugged her knees. He was ready to leave. *Jormungand* hung by the door next to the bag with all his belongings, the rolled up sleeping fur, and the humble hoard—a tidy row for a man who liked order and could leave in an instant.

She wound long russet threads around her fingers and snapped them off her hem. "But there's something you want to say first."

The toe of his boot kicked a dirt clod. Whatever was on his mind had to be excruciating. The beast was tightly coiled. Lines framed the flat line of his mouth as if what he wanted to bite back what he was about to say.

"I love you, Sestra. With all my heart—"

She inhaled fast and sprang off the bed. "I love you, too." She sprinted across the longhouse. Pushing up on her toes, she flung her arms around his neck and rained kisses on his face. New whiskers scraped her lips, the abrasion perfect as she spoke against his jaw, "I'm ready to go to Gotland."

Brandr's body stiffened against her. Her mouth stilled skin tasting of river water. He didn't yield to the moment and fold her into his arms.

Firm hands gripped her arms. "You're not going with me."

"Why not?"

Pain flashed in his grey eyes. "Because I have nothing to give."

"What?" Her heels hit the ground.

Stale silence hung between them as she digested his words. Brandr's Adams apple bobbled and he had the grace to look away. Little by little her arms slid free of him, though her body could be whiplashed. One moment he said the most perfect words, and in the next, he crushed her. She could be back in the island stream for the numbness in her legs.

"That," he said, jabbing his chin at the measly row of things by the door. "Is all I have to offer."

"You have everything to offer me...you *are* everything."

Shoulders rounding forward, his arms crossed tightly over his chest. "Look around you. I can't give you a place to live." His gaze bounced off the rafters overhead. "Not even an empty longhouse."

"Do you think that matters to me?"

"Winter's coming," he said, every inch a hard Viking. "It will matter when the best shelter I provide matches what we had on the island."

"I don't understand, your shipbuilding on Gotland, won't that be enough?"

Fingertips digging into his arms, Brandr stared past the open door, and a new higher wall wedged itself around him. A raven landed on the cauldron shard resting on ashes. The quiet unnerved her more than the clamor of a raid. No matter what Brandr's answer was, she'd lost the man she loved before he was even hers to claim.

"There is a...*requirement*."

She swallowed the dryness in her throat. "You mean a woman."

The skin tightened around his eyes. "Yes."

"Is this what you want?"

Brandr turned, his silver eyes pinning her. "No. I want you."

Her knees buckled but she caught herself, setting a hand over her belly. Why did he have to say beautiful words on one hand and ugly words on the other? He was gutting her one simple statement at a time. Brandr was never fluid with words, but she deserved more than this.

"I don't understand," she said raising an imploring hand. "Please explain yourself better."

"It's simple. I have no land. No means to take care of you save my sword. I'd sell it but where would we be if I had no weapon to defend you?"

"We would make do."

"With battles rising like the tides these days? Not a chance," he scoffed. "Until the question of who sits on the throne is settled, more trouble such as what we faced on the island will come."

"But—"

"In the best of times a man should never be without his weapons," he snapped.

Her breath raced. "You'd rather have security and be with the wrong woman than be with me?"

He leaned a shoulder against the shutter, his eyes a touch mocking. "Didn't you tell Ella it's better to have security with a wealthy master than forge a life on your own?"

"You heard me?"

"I've heard a good many things you've said."

"That's not fair!" But, it was true. She'd said that and spouted similar words all summer long.

"Is it unfair because you're a woman? Because you were born a slave? What makes life fair for the likes of us?"

Chin dipping, she wrapped both arms around her waist. Scalding tears stung her eyes, threatening to spill. "I'm not that woman anymore. Because of you."

"No. Because of you."

She raised her head to meet sharp, all-seeing eyes. She pressed the heels of her hands to her eyes. Brandr knew what it was to claw his way back from dark, degraded places. He was on his way to making a better place for himself when this thing between them happened.

"You changed, became stronger, became a woman of courage all on your own," he went on. "*You* did that, Sestra. No one can lay claim to your bravery, your will…those were gifts you gave yourself."

She leaned a shoulder on the shutter facing him, and her head slumped against solid wood. Wind riffled through long grass where sheep once roamed. She'd visited Lord Hakan's farm when it thrived this past summer, and in the blink of an eye, lives were changed. These troubled times stole the farm of a worthy chieftain yet offered her a way out of lifelong enslavement. Nothing here was fair.

Freedom tasted bland in her mouth if she couldn't be with Brandr.

She stared at the lonely fields outside, hot, churning bile roiling in her stomach. "Tell me about her."

"Sestra," he chided.

"Do you love her?"

Her eyes bored into him. Primal emotions pushed her. No matter how painful, she wanted details. She'd gambled on hope and lost again. This was what happens when she spoke her deepest wishes aloud.

"No." His mouth clamped a hard line as if refusing to give more, but her furious glare must've prodded the stubborn warrior.

Sighing, he explained, "Last spring, Hakan bid me to stay at his ringed fort near Paviken, on Gotland. He was taking his last voyage before settling in to farm here."

"The voyage that brought me to Uppsala."

"Yes," he said, eyeing the fields. "If I'd been with him, all would be different, wouldn't it?"

"It's like a test."

The small line slanted hard between his brows. "One I've failed."

"You've wanted to build ships like Egil for a long time, haven't you?" she asked quietly.

"Yes. Thought about it every day when I trudged through ibn Dawla's fight yard."

"What happened last spring?"
"I ran into Grete, Egil's widow in Paviken. She was overjoyed to see me."

Her body jerked off the shutter. "She doesn't expect you to serve her as slave again? Not after all you've been through?"

"No. She welcomed me to her home. Treated me like a son. I shared what had happened in the years since I last saw her. We both shed tears of sadness over Egil, but she'd long since remarried. To another shipbuilder."

Sestra stared past the open shutters at the fields, folding her arms on the bottom frame. Brandr's feet shifted the subtle sound loud in the cavernous longhouse. In her side vision, he stood beside her, his hand gripping the wooden frame near her elbow.

"Grete's husband is long in years but he has a daughter—"

"Of course he does." She rolled her eyes, and Brandr waited.

A gentle breeze blew wisps of hair across her face, and she saw green fields through a haze of red. If survival was a need, love was pure want. His tale of wants and needs poured salt on a new wound; one she suspected would never fully heal.

"He asked if I'd consider marrying her," he finished.

Men and women married all the time for lesser reasons. Love was a luxury, and she was still a slave. It'd be unwise to get drunk on too much freedom.

"I was promised half his forest as a dowry," he said. "A longhouse had already been built inland on a river. He vowed the rest of the forest would be mine when he dies."

"A fine prize. No wonder you took it."

Instant wealth and stature. What former slave wouldn't grab the opportunity?

"I still had the matter of my service to Hakan. I said I'd consider the offer."

She turned to him. "Then you haven't accepted."

"No. I couldn't get a certain flame-haired thrall out of my mind." His voice was hoarse as he reached over to twist a floating curl floating around his finger.

"Why did you never say anything to me?" Her lips pursed. "Except to insult me for flirting, laziness, and a sharp-tongue."

"I thought it was a matter of lust," he said, his thumb stroking the curl "And more importantly, I wanted you *to want* your freedom."

"Now I want you." She stood before him, heart open. "I would easily trade everything for you."

Did he not understand the power of what they shared? Love wasn't a transaction done between merchants. It was bigger and grander, the whole of it immeasurable. That's what made the emotion perfect. Love was free yet was the most costly thing in the world.

His brow darkened at the humble declaration. He ran his fingers over the long red curl and let go. "First, I need to feed you."

"Brandr—"

He set one finger on her lips. "Food first. Words can wait."

Because he'd take care of her. Brandr gave his all when he looked after others.

He strapped his sword across his back. "Keep an ear open for Hakan's men."

His footsteps light, Brandr disappeared into the forest of trees behind the longhouse. Lord Hakan's home had been built into the knoll, its roof covered in grass.

She touched his hudfat, burying her nose in coarse fur. His smell lingered on the sleeping fur and on his leather bag, his scent fresh like wind and water and pine trees. From his bag, the springy aroma of mint leaves wafted from the bag's narrow opening.

She wandered the length of the longhouse, finishing her braid. For all her relaxed nature, idleness felt wrong. She settled on the earthen floor to sharpen her knife on a makeshift whetstone from the fire pit. With a steady hand, she slid the small stone over her blade. Orange cinders glowed amidst ashes beside her. Up and down the stone sharpened iron, the action soothing. There had to be a way to convince Brandr to forge a life with her.

185

If her palm full bought her freedom, wouldn't his be enough for a good start? Not enough to build ships, but to start a good life.

The whetstone poised over her small blade when hooves pounded outside the longhouse. She jumped up, dropping the rock. Feet rooted to the ground, her attention locked onto the open, sunny lintel. She hid the knife in the folds of her skirt. In the yard, iron rings clanked. It was the thunderous jangle of metal ornaments Vikings put on their horses for battle.

The noised chilled her spine. She'd heard the sound...in Cherbourg.

In the Dane's slave camp.

Brandr crouched behind the tree. Through the leaves he counted Gorm with ten riders. Where was Sestra? Sweat beaded on his forehead. He glanced at the river. No boats. He checked the forest line beyond the rye field. Nothing moved.

Where were Hakan's men?

The Dane pointed at the barn. "You three search the barn, the weaving shed, all the outbuildings." He waved his arm toward the forest beyond the fields. "You three. Check the forest." Shading his eyes, he studied the Fyris before notching his head that way. "The two of you, go to the river and see if you find any signs of boats in the sand."

Hardened fighters galloped their horses across the fields to the forest, the others veered to the river. Three men jumped off their horses, striding through the yard. One knelt by the broken cauldron piece. He sifted through the ashes of yesterday's fire. He swiped a hand through the center of the broken metal and sniffed his fingertips.

"Gorm. I smell food cooked here." His tongue tasted one finger. "Rabbit stew. Possibly yesterday."

The Dane circled his horse around the man crouched by the cauldron. He scanned the line of trees by the longhouse. "They could be hiding in those trees. Keep looking."

Had Sestra climbed through the shutter openings? Brandr spied no movement below the knoll.

The Dane spoke in low tones to a bulky man. The man turned to the forest, his beady eyes narrowing. The Red Bearded man of Aland, the one who ogled Sestra.

Sweat trickled down Brandr's temple. Sven had his spies, the Dane had his.

Noises came from the barn and the weaving shed. One man ransacked the weaver's shed, tossing out a broken loom. Broken pottery shards shattered in the yard. Foolish warrior. He wouldn't last long with his lanky swagger and puffed out chest.

"Could you be any louder?" the Dane called from atop his brown warhorse. "If Hakan's men were coming down river, you've just announced our presence." Gorm jabbed a thumb at the longhouse. "Check in there. *Quietly*."

Sestra.

Brandr dropped to the ground. He inched along on his belly, *Jormungand* in one hand, his knife in the other. If he rolled off the other side of the roof away from the yard…

A scream rent the air.

"Get your hands off me, you filthy swine." Sestra.

187

The lanky warrior led her out of the longhouse, her braid wrapped twice around his hand, a small leather bag clutched in the other. "Look here, Lord Gorm. A woman—" He paused, jerking her braid with one hand, shaking the treasure hoard with the other. "—and the silver you're after."

"Give it here." Gorm cupped his hands to receive the leather bag the warrior tossed up to him. The Dane hefted the bag in one hand, the metal clinking. "Not much is left."

"Could be the woman knows what happened to the rest." Red Beard folded his hands on the pommel.

Gorm raised the bag. "Either way, your payment for spying, as agreed." And he lobbed it Red Beard.

Red Beard frowned at the bag. "Let me at the woman."

"Not yet." Gorm nudged his steed forward, closer to the longhouse doorway where Sestra struggled against the lanky warrior.

Brandr inched along the roof, the grass covering muffling sound well. Three men were deep in the forest. Two searched the riverfront on foot. Five men here in the yard plus Gorm.

Ibn Dawla's voice cracked with an ancient bahadur lesson. *Cut off the head of a snake, and his tail is harmless.*

His belly rubbing grass, his boot toes dug into the roof, scooting him little by little.

Get Gorm. Save Sestra. Get Gorm. Save Sestra.

The rhythm flowed through his veins. Blood pounded in his ears. Gorm badgered Sestra with questions. He couldn't see her but her cries pierced his heart. He loved her more than life.

More than ships and land and promised wealth.

Sun beat down on him. A bead of sweat trickled down his temple. The three men led their horses toward the longhouse, jesting crudely about the curvy flame-haired thrall. His teeth gnashed hard. He'd kill them all. *Get Gorm. Get Sestra.*

Her tearful words carried, "No. I'm here alone. Brandr left me."

He flinched. Her words sliced him. He'd vowed to protect her, yet this morning had one foot almost out the door.

"Yet, his belongings are here and his sword is not." Gorm. The crown of his red hair shined in the sun. "I'll ask again, where is the scout? And where is Hakan?"

"I don't know anything. I'm a thrall," she cried.

Slap. The crack of flesh on flesh burned him. He was ready to drop on the Dane and cut his throat.

"You're a thrall who's forgotten her place. I won't—" *Slap. Slap.* "—ask again."

Five men gathered around Gorm, entertained by the woman kneeling in the dirt. None paid attention to their surroundings. Copper spurted across his tongue. Every muscle tensed for the leap.

Brandr pushed off his hands and knees. He dropped on Gorm, and they tumbled in the yard. *Jormungand* rattled on the ground, coming loose in his grip.

His knife swiveled in his sweat-slick palm. He sliced the Dane's forearm, but his tenacious enemy took the pain and jabbed an elbow into his ribs. *Crack.* Sharp pain. Near the bruise he'd got on the island. Air whooshed from his lungs. Dirt smeared his lips.

The Dane rolled them, yelling, "*Seize him!*"

Beefy hands clamped his arms, jerking him upright. Panting, he strained with all his might for Sestra. She stood, crying, both hands covering her mouth.

"Put a rope around his neck," Gorm ordered, swiping off his trousers.

A warrior tossed a rope around Brandr's neck.

"No!" Agony wrenched Sestra's tear-stained face. She lunged for him only to be caught short, her head snapping back from the cruel warrior holding her by her braid.

Rough hemp scratched his throat. White pain came with the stinging feel of a rope around his neck. The last time was in Sousse.

The warrior holding the rope chucked harshly, kicking Brandr until his knees hit the dirt. His head jerked in time to harsh hands pulling behind him, hands fashioning a knot, cinching it tight against his nape.

Sestra's eyes rounded. Her gaping mouth moved as if she tried to speak but couldn't. She shook from head to toe worse than when cold mist and the stout warrior assaulted her on the island.

The woman he loved looked into his eyes and she knew.

This was the end.

The canny warrior who'd tested the cauldron hefted *Jormungand*. Sunlight gleamed off the bronze etching. "A fine sword."

Gorm wrapped linen around his arm. "It's yours." Blood seeped wide and vivid red on the white linen.

Brandr eyed the sword. Its loss hit him in the gut. The cost of his foolish warrior's choices. He'd failed Odin's test, but Sestra would pay the highest price and be counted of little value. Women always faced this when warriors, good and bad, played their battle games.

His chest heaved. "You have the sword and the treasure. Let her go."

"Let her go?" Gorm laughed, stretching his arm out for one of the warriors to tie a knot. "I can't do that. Mabon is upon us. Harvest End. Tomorrow night. We'll need many to serve in the feast hall. Haven't you heard? I'm leading Uppsala in the ninth year sacrifice."

Hooves thundered from the pasture. Heads turned to the noise. It was the rest of Gorm's men. He used the split second to slug the warrior on his left. Brandr's body swiveled right, ramming his elbow into the other warrior.

Both doubled over. The warrior behind him yanked the rope around his neck. Air thinned inside him. Both hands flew to the rope. He tried to tug it. Pain screamed inside his neck.

A retch built in his belly, but he slammed a fist on the warrior's instep behind him. He felt and heard the satisfying crunch of bone. The warrior yelped in pain, dropping to the ground.

"Would someone *pl-ease* contain him?" Gorm's voice dripped with long-suffering irritation.

Four men stood over him. Two kicked him. His back. His cheek. His shoulder. His thighs. His arse. Again and again. The tang of copper mixed with the salt of his sweat. Clouds of dust billowed around him, and he'd swear ibn Dawla's laughing black eyes flashed in the haze.

The fight yard...defeat.

"Kill him." Gorm's voice rose above the noise.

"No!" Sestra's scream rattled him.

He'd take his fill of her one more time. She screamed again, iron shining in her hand. Her arm arced wide slashing the fighter's hand gripping her braid. Blood spurted and the long, red braid fell to the ground.

"I said kill him," Gorm commanded.

Jormungand shined overhead. Brandr tried to move, but boots pinned his wrists to the yard and one drove a boot on his ankle. White hot pain jabbed his ribs, his legs. His cheek in the dirt, the sun blinded him when he lifted his head. The men laughed cruelly as he moaned.

Another warrior held the viper sword high to deliver the ultimate dishonor, a blood eagle death by a warrior's own sword.

A soft, feminine body launched on top of him.

"Sestra..." Dry dust and blood coated his mouth.

One eye pinched from flesh swelling fast, but she pressed her cheek into the earth, facing him. Red curls blossomed around her face, her hair shorn around her shoulders. Tears washed over freckles he'd once kissed. She used her body to shield him. The ache of her will to sacrifice for him cut to core.

She tried to save him. His brave *Sif*....

Dirty fingers snatched her by the shoulders, pulling her off his body. Another hand wrenched the knife from her fist.

His throat thick dirt and defeat, he opened his mouth to say he loved her. Her wails pierced the air as *Jormungand* flashed high.

"Wait." Gorm raised a staying hand. "Tomorrow night is the Feast of Mabon. Don't we need a ninth man to sacrifice to Odin?"

Chapter Fourteen

"You still don't know who bought you?" Ella dragged a pitcher through ale.

"You think I'm concerned with who bought me?" Sestra hissed under her breath. "When Brandr's about to face *that*?" She nodded at a table draped with white linen stretched before the king's chair, a freshly forged knife gleaming in the middle. "I won't let it happen."

The king's great hall hummed with House Karls and shield maidens, highborn men and women, their children nestled close. The hall's oak doors were thrown wide to show a small green field lit by blazing torches. An ancient gnarled tree reigned; its tangled branches spread high and wide.

Inside the Dane held court, having spared nothing for Mabon, a minor blot for Vikings, but for him the grand pronouncement, he was King of Svea.

Gorm sat on the king's ornately carved chair with two Norse hammers crossed at the handles on the wall above his head. Beside him, stiff as the ice-queen many claimed her to be, was Lady Astrid of Uppsala, former wife of Lord Hakan.

Lord Hakan. Sestra's mouth twisted bitterly as she filled more pitchers with ale. Brandr had done everything in his power to fulfill his oath to the chieftain. And his reward? Gorm's men dragged Brandr away to live one more day in an outbuilding in Uppsala, separated from others because he was Lord Hakan's prized scout.

At midnight, Brandr would be sacrificed on the pristine table, and his body taken to hang upside on Uppsala's great tree.

Ella set a calming hand on her arm. "I'm sorry. I'm just as frightened as you by all that's happened."

Frightened? Fear mingled with nerve-rattling anger. Despite her servitude today, the woman who kept her mouth and stayed out of the way was long gone. A heavy weight lodged in her stomach. She couldn't eat, couldn't drink because her mind was consumed with how to save Brandr.

She refused to sink into despair. The Viking bahadur wouldn't have. He'd patiently work a solution.

Elle wiped her eyes, a red welt blooming on her cheek. The young thrall was alone and scared. Lady Henrikkson had fled Uppsala, and now Ella was under the rule of an unkind matron from Hedeby.

Sestra wrapped an arm around her shoulder. "I'm sorry. I don't want to frighten you."

"These are frightening times," Ella said bravely. "I want to help."

"I can't ask that of you." She eyed the shield maidens sitting shoulder to shoulder with the men. Thralls bustled around tables set end to end around the longhouse. Hundreds of feasting revelers crammed the hall.

The midnight sacrifice was a few hours away.

Ella squared her shoulders and tossed back her black braid. "Someone has already asked me to help." She ducked her head close. "I have a message from Emund, Lord Hakan's warrior."

Sestra's head turned sharply. "What? Where is he?"

"He grabbed me when I went outside to gather more fire wood. He's waiting for you in the trees behind the feasting hall."

"Now?"

"Yes. Now," Ella hissed, jerking her head at the back door.

Her breaths came fast and shallow. She rubbed high on her chest where hope blossomed painfully. There'd been too many horrible disappointments. She was ready to take matters into her own hands.

"Finally the chieftain's here," she muttered.

"And you will let me help." Ella set a firm hand on Sestra's arm, her blue eyes brittle. "Even if it means death."

"I've a plan," she said snatching her cloak off a peg on the wall. "And you won't have to die for it."

Ella glared at the tables where boisterous laughter rose. "Anything to rid Uppsala of these invaders."

"Good. Can you get men's trousers and a tunic? Both in black? Bring them to me behind the feasting hall with a pitcher of ale and two drinking horns."

"What if Emund wants to take you to safety? Will you flee?"

"Not until Brandr's safe." Her mouth firmed.

Sestra raised the black wool hood high on her head. Three rips in the cloak were all that remained of Brandr using it as a weapon on the island. Another thing she'd learned from the Viking bahadur: everything was a weapon for the mind smart enough to see the possibility.

Now it was her turn to use her cunning.

Ella donned her cloak. "You *do* love him. But you're no warrior. You've never touched a sword a day in your life."

She smiled grimly at the throne. "There's more than one to win a fight."

If the plan didn't work…she set a quelling hand on her belly. She wouldn't think of that. She'd take her chances on this last hope. It was all she had left.

Chapter Fifteen

Flames guttered as Sestra darted past the last torch staked in the ground. The strong resin smell followed her as she climbed a knoll and walked into the pitch black forest behind the king's hall. Leaves crunching underfoot, she slowed her steps to let her eyes adjust to the dark.

Music drifted from the hall, and she halted mid-step to listen. Goat bone flutes trilled deceptively light-hearted notes, preparing revelers for the awful hour sacrifices would begin. When drums pounded, it'd be time for the men.

She clutched her skirts and picked up the pace to find Emund. Her mind raced with the bold plan. If every part didn't fall into place; if others didn't follow through as expected....

If. If. If. What would worry get her?

A tall, cloaked form slipped from behind a tree ahead, and she froze. Hands pushed back the hood, revealing carrot orange hair.

"Emund?" she whispered.

"I'm here."

She scurried deeper into the line of trees and Gunnar popped out from behind a bush. He too was cloaked. Emund scanned his surroundings, and satisfied they were safe, he started pulling her behind a tree.

She grabbed his arm. "Wait. Ella is coming."

"Gunnar," Emund notched his head toward the feasting hall. "Go wait for Ella and bring her to the stone clearing."

Emund led her uphill further into the woods to a place with two sizeable rocks. He bid her take a seat, and he did the same beside her. Through the trees, smoke billowed high and thick from the hall's smoke hole. Torches burning around Uppsala's ancient tree glowed beautifully like shining amber pieces on black cloth.

The warrior's eyes glittered sadly in the moonlight. "We waited for you at Lord Hakan's farm."

"Not long enough."

He looked away, suitably chastened. Brandr was a respected fighter of notable skill. Emund's young shoulders drooped under his cloak as if he alone bore the burden of responsibility. If he'd been there, Brandr would have gone safely away from Uppsala instead of sitting tied up, waiting to be sacrificed.

She shuddered. Vikings could be beautiful and fierce yet so brutal.

And because Emund wasn't waiting for them, she had another night with Brandr. Her rough bahadur declared his love for her, and she for him, but the gift of more time together came at too high a price.

Emund scrubbed both hands through his hair. "Everything fell apart after you left. One of Sven's Aland warriors turned out to be a spy for Gorm."

"I know. The one with the red beard."

"Einar." He sighed. "Suddenly everyone tried to flee Uppsala. It was chaos, trying to help people escape. Gorm came with all his men and set fire to much of Uppsala. What was left, he gifted to his followers who arrived from Jutland today."

"The plan to divide his forces didn't work," she mused, her fingers holding back the side of her hood.

From this place in the woods, she viewed the charred remains of what once was Uppsala's market place where foreign traders pitched tents to hawk their wares. Homes of Viking craftsmen were gone. Frosunda known for fashioning the finest elk bone needles, the silversmith, the glass maker who formed beads of every color, all manner of goods and people...lost.

Foreigners vanished at the first whiff of trouble. Not Uppsala's merchants. They were either dead or gone, their homes and livelihoods scorched in the Dane's grasp for power.

"Gorm stole many ships to stop people from leaving." Emund pointed deeper into the forest. "He stores the vessels in the north inlet belonging to Lady Astrid. Gifts for the Black Wolf's men when they come."

She pushed off the rock and marched to an opening in the trees. Facing north, she spied scattered outbuildings. "And despite his efforts to stop the Dane, Brandr's tied up."

Emund stared at the moonlit harbor. "Waiting to die."

"He won't die," she said, sharply. "And you're going to help him escape."

"How? Lord Hakan won't be here until dawn." He nodded at the harbor where a moonbeam split the blackness. "That's when Sven arrives with ships and reinforcements from Aland."

Sestra drummed her fingers on the tree trunk, keeping an eye on one building in particular. Emund was a gentle soul who always followed orders. He was entrusted to care for her and Helena on Lord Hakan's ship when they journeyed as thralls to Uppsala. A newly minted warrior, Emund had served the chieftain for little more than a year. The young Viking likely didn't know about Brandr's rescue from a galley ship years ago.

Nor did he know he faced a rebellious woman who'd risk all for the man she loved.

"For now, the harbor is empty of rescuers. No one else is here but us." She pivoted on her heel to face him "We'll follow my plan to save Brandr."

"How?"

Footsteps brushed through leaves from Gunnar and Ella trotting fast. Gunnar carried the pitcher and two drinking horns.

Ella held out folded black clothes. "I have the clothes."

"How you ask? With these for a start," she said, taking the clothes from Ella. "Now both of you turn around. Ella, help me change my clothes."

Gunnar obliged her request, but Emund didn't. He planted both hands on his hips and pressed her.

"What's your plan?" he asked testily. "As I see it the moon is less than an hour from midnight and the four of us are sorely outnumbered."

Her breath came faster. Time was running out. New instruments joined the bone flutes, a sign Mabon's celebration picked up speed. She untied her boots and toed them off. Ella picked them up, and Sestra stepped into the moonlight all the better to see what she was doing. Men had gawked at her with less than night to cover her skin.

In one fluid motion she dropped her cloak. "Ella will distract the guard."

The slave girl nodded. "I can do that."

Sestra whipped the tattered tunic over her head, adding, "When she does, you and Gunnar will walk out of the outbuilding with Brandr."

Gunnar spoke over his shoulder. "A bold plan, but what happens when the guard finds his captive's gone?"

She traded her tunic for trousers and pulled them up over her hips. Her bottom wiggled...such freedom in trousers. "He won't."

"You can't be sure," Emund said, watching her lace up the trousers. "He'll raise the alarm—"

"When the alarm is sounded it'll be too late," she said and raised her arms for Ella to drop a roomy man's tunic over her head. When her face cleared the neckline, she finished, "You'll have taken Brandr far away from here. Gorm won't be able to touch him."

Gunnar turned to face her, the pitcher still in one hand and the drinking horns in the other. "Am I missing something?" He held up the pitcher. "I doubt this is enough ale to get the man drunk."

"Ella, my boots." Sestra crouched down and slipped one boot on and then the other. "The ale is enticement for the guard to sit with Ella." she said, her fingers flying over the garters.

"What happens when the guard finds Brandr gone?" Emund asked his voice suspicious.

Sestra stood up and gathered her hair at her nape. "He won't."

Ella handed her a leather thong to bind her hair. Both men looked to the other, frowns writ on their faces.

"This is a bad idea," Gunnar began.

"It's the only idea." Hair secured, she put on her cloak.

Emund lunged forward and grabbed her arm. "You want to take his place."

He glared fiercely at her, his hand a manacle on her arm. Carrot-haired Emund appeared to have more bite than she'd first thought.

"I *will* take his place," she said, her chin tipping high.

His sky blue eyes measured her before he let go. "We can't promise that we'll be able to save you."

"I know."

"What?" Gunnar stepped around Emund. "You can't be serious. Don't you want to live?"

Her chest rose and fell with labored breaths. She'd done no more than changed her clothes but the way her heart pounded she could've charged a steep hill. She had to wait until mead and Frankish wine flowed heavily inside the king's hall. The celebrations would cloud their minds and slow reactions. For the all the revelry going on, the Dane would hold the sacrifices much later in the night. Music throbbed, louder with more instruments.

A lone warrior walked out from the shadows to the ancient tree. The man blew on Uppsala's bronze lur, the long single note blast causing a roar to erupt inside the hall.

Emund's face turned stony. "They're sounding the call for war. With our own horn."

"Doesn't that make you want revenge for what they've done to Uppsala?" She said quietly.

"I do." The feminine voice spoke up in the darkness.

All heads turned to Ella. Night's pale light shined on glossy jet black hair. Her fragile profile was as soft and white as the moon. The welt showed a purple beside her ear as she glowered at Uppsala's ruins.

"And we don't have much time," the sweet thrall said with all finality.

"I want to live," Sestra said but her throat tight. "As much as I want Brandr to live." "You have my vow that I will do everything I can to come back for you. I don't know how, but I will," Gunnar promised.

His glower reminded her of her fierce, tied up Viking.

"Thank you, but if something happens—" Her voice cracked and she cupped her mouth, holding back a cry. "If something happens, please tell him that I want him to live to build his ships on Gotland."

Ella rubbed her shoulder. "Shhh," the maid cooed. "If they don't tell your brave warrior, I will."

Sestra didn't want to die. Strange numbness came with the certainty of what she was about to do. She'd faced death on the island and won. Was it too much to hope she'd outsmart it again?

Clearing her throat, she stood tall. "We don't have much time. Are we ready?"

Three pairs of eyes glittered back at her in darkness. Emund's eyes glowed with newfound respect as did Gunnar's. Ella, though, surprised her most of all. Sprite-blue eyes hardened like sapphire stones, a willing shield maiden in the face of death.

The walk to the barn was quiet. Acrid smells of singed wood filled the air. Thin curls of smoke twisted from the ruins of once proud longhouses. In the Dane's effort to put on a fine feast for his Jutland friends, he ordered thralls to round up animals for the feast. With the herds already culled, food stores plundered, and fields neglected, winter would prove severe. Jogging to Uppsala's farthest structures, she suspected King Gorm would ensure his Jutland friends ate while Uppsala's people starved.

The outbuilding was ahead, wide gaps showing between wood slats. A lone warrior guarded the door, a nasty bearded axe tipped over his shoulder.

Sestra tapped Emund's shoulder, and whispered. "Ella will approach him. If all goes well, she will lead him to sit with her by the blacksmith's forge."

He nodded. "I see it."

"You and Gunnar will come with me to the barn. Both of you will take Brandr away."

"Are you certain you want to do this?" Gunnar asked. His features were tense and pleading. "Brandr will fight this when he sees us."

"He won't. The guards drugged him when they separated him from the other men to be sacrificed. He was causing too much trouble."

Gunnar's gaze shot to the huge blond guard standing wide-legged in front of the doorway. "You have black clothes but your hair...the red will give you away."

She shook her head. "Brandr wears a hood. All the men to be sacrificed do. I'll put it over my head and you can put my cloak on Brandr. No one will be the wiser."

"You're hardly the same size and shape as him," he scoffed.

"It's dark and there are no torches here. By the time it's discovered I'm a woman, you'll be long gone."

A shiver like bony fingers traced her spine. The blot was for men only to be offered to Odin, not women. Woman or not, her fate was sealed when the Dane rode into Lord Hakan's farm.

"Decide now if you're in or not," she said. "But don't argue. This is my choice."

"She's right." Emund's face showed stern in the shadows.

"We don't have any more time to argue. I'm ready." Ella didn't wait.

She padded off to the end of the alley, the pitcher in one hand, drinking horns grasped between thumb and forefinger of the other. The ebon haired thrall paused, straightened her spine, before putting one foot in front of the other.

Hips swaying, braid curved over her shoulder, Ella's raven tresses shined in moonlight, her seductive saunter a garment she wore with ease. She greeted the guard, her giggle infectious and sweet. The Viking smiled back, fingering a wide bronze band clasped around the middle of his beard. The guard didn't stand a chance against Ella's feminine assault.

The pair strolled to the blacksmith's shop where Ella made sure the Viking's back was to the outbuilding—all the better to see the road to the feast hall when men would come for the captive to be offered.

Sestra and the men scurried into the outbuilding. Brandr was the only chattel inside. Tied to the center post, his hands were bound behind his back. She ran to him, her heart filling her throat, and pulled the russet hood off his head.

One bruised eye fluttered half open as far as it would go. The other had swelled shut. "Sestra…" he stirred half-unconscious, mumbling her name.

"Shhhh." She kissed him on the mouth. His lips were cracked and dry. All visible skin was bruised and battered. She kissed him again and spoke against the shell of his ear. "If you remember anything from tonight, know this. I love you."

Blood caked his torn tunic to his chest. His less bruised eyelid quavered.

She touched the longer shaggy curl on his neck. "My rules say: You deserve a second chance."

Emund sawed the ties binding his hands and when the last binding gave, Brandr moaned.

His hands flopped to his sides covered in dried blood.

"You tried to break free from your bindings, same as on the ship." Her voice was brittle to her ears.

Brandr's ribs expanded with shallow breaths. He raised a shaky hand but the effort must've been too much. His hand fell to his lap.

"Get him out of here," she said, a lump growing in her throat.

Gunnar linked his arms around Brandr and hauled him up from behind. "Come with us. We can make it," he said, looking down at her as she took her place against the post.

"Emund, tie my hands and put the hood on my head."

Brandr's head lolled forward and his legs were limp as rags. He was completely out.

"This is foolhardy," Gunnar said, struggling to hold up Brandr.

She faced forward and put both hands behind her back. "If I go with you, the guard will return and see no one here. He'll sound the alarm and all of Gorm's men will scour the forest and capture us all." She angled her head at Gunnar. "You know I'm right."

Crouched beside her, Emund wound leather around her wrists. "The knots will be loose," he said close to her ear. He set the hood on her head and waited. "When we get Brandr to safety, we will try to come for you. I don't know how, but we will."

"We will," Gunnar said firmly.

"Keep this in your mouth." Emund held up a dried mushroom. "If we don't make it in time…" his words trailed off.

She eyed the tough as leather piece. "Put it in my mouth."

Emund slipped it past her lips. Her tongue rolled the mushroom to the side of her mouth.

"It will deaden any pain and make you feel as if you're floating in water."

Floating in water. How perfect. Her closed-lipped smile stretched and she glanced at the hood. Emund tucked the wool under her chin. Through the weave, three forms struggled to move with stealth.

Had she dragged undeserving people into her desperate plan? Ella's giggle carried on the wind. Footsteps trod the earthen floor, getting fainter, quieter, until she heard them no more.

Brandr was gone.

Head tipped back against the beam, her teeth ground the leathery mushroom in her mouth. There was no reason to wait for the Dane's wrath to find escape from pain. Her eyes stung, and the harder she chewed the farther she sunk into a chasm of despair. Emund and Gunnar wouldn't come back. They couldn't. Emund accepted this, not Gunnar with his forceful protests.

One tear rolled down her cheek as she waited for the mushroom to take effect. Not even an other-worldy shade would sit with her in this quest to save the man she loved. She rested her head on the wooden beam and waited. Rich music from the king's hall played, the melody reaching a fevered pitch. The drums were about to begin.

She was alone, and she was going to die alone.

Chapter Sixteen

Wolfish ice blue eyes peered into hers. Her stomach heaved, but she didn't retch.

Big hands pulled up her eyelids. "She's alive."

The big hands grabbed her by the waist. A large man tossed her over his shoulder, and her head flopped loosely from the jolt. Long legs ranged forward and she bobbed with each step the man made. Darkness and flames everywhere. Her eyes tried to open. She moaned. A wall of heat hit her face. Uppsala was burning.

She tried to move but a big arm clamped hard over her thighs. "Don't move. It's better that way."

Her cracked lips refused to cooperate. Wool could be stuffed inside her mouth for all the dryness there. She tried to move her tongue but it stuck to the roof of her mouth.

"Don't talk either. All you need to know is my wife required me to move heaven and earth to get you."

She squinted but her grainy eyes couldn't focus. The voice…familiar but a haze closed in on all sides of her vision until she saw no more.

* * *

Sunlight pierced her eyes. She narrowed them to thin slits, the brightness too much to take. A sleeping fur, smelling of Brandr tickled her nose. The eiderdown bed...

No. This bed rocked.

Brandr. Deep ache welled up in her chest. Wind brushed her cheeks as if to dry waiting tears. The cry rolled through her body and passed through parted lips. She was alone. Chin quivering, she was alone.

"Oh Sestra. You're awake." A warm hand folded over hers. The gentle voice spoke Norse but with a Frankish lilt.

"Helena?"

"It is I." Helena angled her head, blocking out the sun. "Is that better?"

She nodded and touched her temple. "Hammers bang inside my head."

"The effects of the mushroom Emund gave you. You'll have tiredness, and your head will ache. Emotions may overwhelm you."

Her thick tongue filled her mouth. Of course the apothecary's daughter would know these things.

"W-water?"

"Yes." Helena dribbled wetness from a water pouch on the corner of her mouth. "Not too much or your stomach will heave it back up again."

The sweet trickle flooded her tongue. Her eyes opened wider. "Brandr?"

It hurt to say his name, but if she lived, he must've survived. The warrior likely took the first boat to his new life

211

on Gotland. One day their paths would cross. He'd be angry but grateful for what she did, and the fast, hot love she'd seen in his eyes will have faded with his newfound wealth. And his wife.

She winced.

"What's wrong?" Helena leaned in, wiping a cool cloth to her head.

Sestra shook her head, a bare nudge since she didn't want to move. The world around her lurched, and she set her hand on the plank beside her. Seagulls flew overhead.

"Boat?"

"Yes. We're on a fishing boat headed for Gotland. We're almost there."

She burrowed deeper in the sleeping fur. Briny air filled her lungs. Slapping sounds touched her ear, water tapping the side of the boat.

Helena kept up her tender ministration, wiping her cheeks and forehead. "You are the bravest woman I know. Your advice saved my life."

Her brows knit. Flashes of the past jarred her aching head…of them sitting in Cherbourg, waiting as slaves to be purchased. Helena, at least, became treasured wife of a chieftain.

"Don't you remember?" Helena asked. "'Those that fight don't live long.' You were right. I didn't fight the path laid before me. I embraced it." Dark blue eyes sparkled. "With some troubles along the way."

She rested on the fur. When she was better, she'd ask about Brandr. For now, her weak body gave over to Helena's care.

The damp cloth stopped. "I hope you'll forgive me for not telling you this before, but I bought you from Lady Henrikkson. She'd just sent you to help Mardred." Helena's face clouded. "I was on my way to the meet Hakan at Halsten and Mardred's farm when the Aland warriors attacked. He didn't know I'd bought you."

Her eyes flew open. Helena leaned close, her long chestnut locks flowing unbound. Helena put the water pouch to Sestra's lips. The cool, healing trickle felt good.

"I did it to set you free."

Her tongue flicked over dry lips, wetting them with the water. "Free?"

"Yes. You're welcome to live on Hakan's Gotland ringed fort...as a freewoman."

"Let me see," she said her voice a hoarse croak. "I offer advice; you buy me to set me free." She laughed softly. "Not a balanced trade."

"Then you're not angry with me for not telling you when I saw you at Mardred's farm?"

"When the Aland warrior held a knife to your neck? You had other things on your mind, such as your tied up husband."

"You are getting better." Helena laughed. "You're humor's back.

"On second thought, my advice landed you a husband. A privileged one at that."

"Men are not all there is to life." Helena's dimple showed in at the corner of her mouth. "But they are a welcome boon. Perhaps, you will find a husband soon?"

She tugged the fur up higher. Her heart was too raw. The organ pumped her blood, its steady rhythm going strong in her chest. Yet, she'd swear that part of her chest wound up into a tight, fierce ball, refusing to uncoil.

"Men will flock to you, Sestra. They always do. You can have your pick of them in Gotland."

Brandr.

She wanted the man who made a fine shelter out of sticks in a forest. The rough-hewn Viking who whispered tender Persian words when he ravaged her body. The man who read the ground, the trees, and water the way scribes read parchment.

"Did he survive his wounds?" She curled her hands in his fur. "And did he make it safely out of Uppsala?"

"He did." Helena smiled and pushed off her seat. She balanced a hand on the ship's rail, crouching on the balls of her feet. "Since you're feeling better, why don't you ask him about his wounds?"

"He's an angry beast most of the time."

"It takes a strong woman to tame a man like him."

"I'm not sure…" She fidgeted, longing for the comfort of sleep. "I will bide my time before I see him on Gotland."

Helena rose to her feet. "You don't have to wait for Gotland. He's here."

She gasped.

Helena stepped over a chest, saying loud enough for all to hear, "He's been waiting to talk to you."

Sunlight blinded her eyes again but with Helena out of the way, black wool outlined broad shoulders rowing in long, gingered strokes. She blinked and shaded her eyes. One tarnished silver eye looked back at her. The other eye was swollen shut and purple. Strips of Brandr's shredded tunic fluttered in the breeze.

Eight men rowed the fishing boat. With no mast, the vessel wasn't meant to cross from Uppsala to Gotland, but these were desperate times. Brandr's one-eyed gaze latched onto her. Tenderness glowed from his eye as did wariness. His Adam's apple bobbled in his throat as he rose from his seat. Stepping with care, he came to her side, folding his big body close to hers.

One rough hand stroked red curls flying across her face. He brushed them back only to have errant sea breezes blow them right back. His patient hand stroked her skin. She could be a treasured piece of finery.

"I promise I won't break," she teased.

"You nearly did." Voice breaking, his good eye flinched.

"I'm glad you're alive." Her arm reached out from the hudfat. She sought any part of him to touch and got his boot-covered calf.

"Thanks to you." His thumb grazed the fat freckle at the side of her mouth.

They stayed that way, him caressing her face and her stroking his boot. Simple things made this dear: sun shining on his black hair, the well-traveled iron amulet swinging over her head, and the fact that he could move at all after the abuse he took.

Her Viking bahadur's face showed awe. Regret. Sorrow. He wanted to speak. She knew it in her bones, but a man like Brandr needed time. When he shared his thoughts they were more precious than silver.

His words would come. She'd wait.

The man-sized tunic she wore rode up under her chin, and she wriggled awkwardly, tugging it down.

"Problem with your clothes?" Brandr's brilliant smile broke wide.

A hiccup of laughter rolled through her. She cupped his jaw, covered with dried blood and new black whiskers. "Is that something you can help with?"

Pain flashed over his features. "Is that something you *want* me to help with?"

"Yes. For the rest of my life," she whispered.

"I'd rather keep you naked in my sleeping fur."

"You're talking to a free woman now. No man will get me in his sleeping furs unless I say so."

His dry chuckle was a beautiful sound. Brandr's good eye softened at the corner. "You are the bravest woman I know. You've saved my life. Twice."

"It was the least I could do since you saved mine once." She tried to keep her words light and playful, but she turned her face, gulping back the grief.

"Sestra," he murmured. "I love you. I was wrong."

She stared at the wood planks inches from her nose. "Wrong to want something better?"

"*You* are my something better," he said fiercely. "You are."

"What about all your fine forests?"

"Nothing compares to you. Nothing. Be my wife and we'll find our way together."

She caressed his whiskers, coaxing him close. "Two former slaves forging their way in the world." His cut mouth hovered over hers. "Sounds dangerous."

He kissed her softly and spoke against her lips, "*Doost-et daaram,* my flame-haired *Sif.* You are my greatest treasure."

Author Notes

Svea. This is modern day Sweden. In the Viking Age, Svea was comprised of the island of Aland, Uppsala and surrounding areas, and the rich island of Gotland.

Uppsala in AD 1022. This was a fascinating year. My *Norse series* is built around historical events of that time, in particular, the exile of King Olof Skotkonung. Good King Olof reigned from 1008 – 1022 and by all accounts was a strong, fair ruler. His bloodless exile really did happen – by his own fully bearded 14 year old son, Anund Jakob (and for the reasons in this book). Olof tried to do away with the 9th year custom of sacrifice, but the people of Uppsala refused. Olof and Jakob were real Vikings. Gorm is pure fiction.

Fyris River. The Fyris River borders one side of Uppsala, but in Viking times was called the Sala River. You can see how Uppsala's name evolved. The river was changed to Fyris in the 1600s. I went with the modern name in case you want to look things up on a map.

Birka. This outpost south of Uppsala is real. However, it died out around AD 960. For fictional reasons, I kept it around a few more decades in this series.

Lake Ekoln. Uppsala is inland with Lake Ekoln the largest body of water it's Viking Age harbor. There are smaller islands within the vast lake, which gave rise to the fictitious island in this story.

Tyrian Purple/Tyrian Red. This was the most highly prized dye in the world. Used for dying royal robes and clothes of the uber-wealthy, people paid dearly for vials of Tyrian. Its value held strong from antiquity through early Middle Ages. A merchant who sold it was called a "seller of purple." Why Tyrian Red and Tyrian Purple? Tyrian refers to someone from the city of Tyre. The colors came from how the biochemical reacted to certain fabrics (some it turned deep purple and with others a rich, black-red). The dye comes the keyhole limpet (a marine gastropod for the science-minded, a sea snail in layman's terms).

Birka and Tyrian Purple feature prominently in another Viking series in the works, The Forgotten Sons. For more Norse series world, check out my website and click on the "Book Worlds" tab.

Catch the first book in the series, *Norse Jewel.*
Coming soon, the third book in the series, *To Heal a Viking Heart*, the tale of the Black Wolf and Gisla, Uppsala's healer.
Last in the series is *To Save a Viking Warrior*, the tale of Katla and Tyrgve

Discover More by Gina Conkle

Midnight Meetings Series (Georgian Romance)
Meet the Earl at Midnight
The Lady Meets Her Match

About the Author

A love of history, books, and romance is the perfect recipe for a historical romance writer. Gina's passion for castles and old places (the older and moldier the better!) means interesting family vacations. Good thing her husband and two sons share similar passions, except for romance…that's where she gets the eye roll. When not visiting interesting places, she can be found in southern California delving into the latest adventures of organic gardening and serving as chief taxi driver

Made in the USA
Columbia, SC
11 December 2017